Sherie took her own coffee and a macaroon, then sat opposite Richard in the grey fabric-covered armchair that matched the couch he had chosen. This was the moment; it would be ridiculous and awkward to put it off any longer. He was already gazing at her, a speculative question in his heavy-lashed blue eyes.

'I think you know why I asked you to come,' she said.

'No, I don't,' he answered, after a gulp of cream-topped coffee. 'Was there a reason? A specific one, I mean?'

'Obviously there was,' Sherie retorted. It was clear that he hadn't decided to make this easy for her, 'I'd scarcely ask a senior doctor to my own flat after less than a week together on the ward without a reason. Please stop this pretence!'

'What pretence, Sister Page?' He was wary now, which was perhaps not surprising. Her tone had begun to betray the underlying hostility she could not rid herself of.

'Richard . . . didn't my name or my face ring any bells when we were introduced?' asked Sherie. 'Haven't they rung any bells since?'

Lilian Darcy lives in Sydney, Australia. As well as romances she also writes for the theatre, films and television, and her interests include winter sports, music and French. She says she writes Medical Romances because it gives her the opportunity to create heroines who are real, who work for their living, care about what they do and lead interesting and fulfilling lives. Although she has had no medical training she has many friends in the profession who delight in providing her with details. They have even been known to get into heated arguments over the exact treatment her hero ought to prescribe!

Previous titles

CALLING AIR DOCTOR THREE
VALENTINES FOR NURSE CLEO

SISTER PAGE'S PAST

BY

LILIAN DARCY

MILLS & BOON LIMITED
ETON HOUSE   18-24 PARADISE ROAD
RICHMOND   SURREY   TW9 1SR

First published in Great Britain 1989
by Mills & Boon Limited

© Lilian Darcy 1989

Australian copyright 1989
Philippine copyright 1989
This edition 1989

ISBN 0 263 76568 7

Set in English Times 11 on 11 pt.
03 – 8910 – 57731

Typeset in Great Britain by JCL Graphics, Bristol

Made and Printed in Great Britain

CHAPTER ONE

'DON'T speak to me like that, please,' It was a clear, confident young voice, resonant with anger, determinedly polite.

Ward Sister Sherie Page winced and looked up from her desk, pushing back a glossy strand of inky black hair from her forehead with an absent hand. Yes, of course it was Alison Grace who had uttered the words.

She stood in the open doorway that led to one of the two single-bed rooms on the ward, and even though her shoulders were set and stiff, her stance had a coltish grace that matched her name. The man who faced her was massive and lumbering by contrast, and his skin was rapidly assuming a mottled reddish hue as he gaped from the sheer shock of the young girl's words.

He was Professor Hindley Thorpe, consultant specialist in surgical oncology, with a world-wide reputation in his field, and first-year nurses like Alison Grace simply did *not* challenge or confront him in any way!

Sherie rose swiftly but reluctantly, the well-proportioned curves of her own figure revealing themselves with the movement. She did not like Professor Thorpe, and there had already been at least two occasions during her three weeks in charge of this ward when she would have loved to use Alison's words to the man—or indeed, something much stronger—but she hadn't and wouldn't, and now it was up to her to smooth over this declaration of hostilities before it escalated into full-scale aggression.

She did not take her eyes from the pair as she skimmed towards them unobtrusively. They both stood speechless—Professor Thorpe through sheer outrage and surprise, and Alison no doubt because her initial bravado had ebbed and she was now feeling completely terrified.

'Please finish what you were doing, and then go and wait for me in the ward conference room, Nurse, I'd like to talk to you,' Sherie said quietly, with a nod and a gesture that were clear signals of dismissal.

Alison tossed her strawberry-blonde head and walked away, heading down the corridor to the far end of the ward. Sherie noted the two spots of defiant colour that still burned on her cheeks, but caught as well a fleeting look of sheer relief in the girl's brown eyes.

'Could I get you some coffee, Professor Thorpe?' Sherie asked winningly.

He turned to her abruptly, opened his mouth to speak, then stopped and stared at her for a moment, with an odd expression. It wasn't attractive, but Sherie had confronted this and similar expressions many times since the age of sixteen when she had suddenly turned from a scruffy, mop-topped and ungainly girl into a strikingly beautiful young woman. Sherie was rarely flattered by this interest. Beauty was said to be skin deep, but to her it seemed that the reactions it produced were even shallower. She did not want to be liked for her looks but for what she was inside. Professor Thorpe, of course, according to hospital mythology, had never been known to like anybody.

'No, Sister,' he said impatiently after a moment, then took in a long rasping breath through his bulbous nose, obviously preparing to launch into some kind of tirade. Sherie waited, her dark sapphire eyes fixed on him calmly. It was all she could do.

The words came, blunt and rude. Generally Professor Thorpe remembered that it was in his own interests to keep Ward Sisters on his side, but when something happened to make him forget, the veneer slipped, and the natural boorishness and insensitivity of the man was revealed.

Idiocy…incompetence…the words pelted on and on, while Sherie nodded, smiled, agreed, or firmly but very, very politely made a point against him. After several minutes, it was finally over.

'I'm late,' Professor Thorpe snapped sharply, and he was gone before Sherie had managed to state that the first-year nurse would *not* be dismissed, nor would all nursing students be kept out of his path in future, nor any pay be docked or written reports submitted on the matter, thank you very much.

She watched him until he had turned into the corridor that led to the lifts, and only then did she realise that her breath was held and her teeth were clenched.

She let her chest relax in a controlled sigh and worked her jaw gently a few times to loosen it. The man was a brilliant surgeon, he had worked a life-time in this field, he had never married and was obsessive in his dedication, she reminded herself. So perhaps it was unreasonable to expert that he be human as well.

And now for Alison Grace…

Lisa Perry, second in command on this shift, smiled at Sherie's harassed expression as they passed each other in the corridor.

'Another disaster, and it's not even lunchtime?'

'Something like that,' Sherie nodded, then she

slipped down the corridor to the end of the ward, choosing not to explain the incident to Lisa at this stage, even in summarised form.

Alison would probably be hiding in the linen store, or perhaps the activities room, and very likely she would be in tears. Best to talk it over with the girl herself first.

Sherie poked her head around each door, her sympathetic smile at the ready, but the rooms were deserted. It was through the next door, one that opened into one of the four-bed rooms, that Alison's bright head could be glimpsed, bent earnestly over a nine-year-old patient's notes.

'Alison…'

She looked up immediately, and the defiant spots of colour glowed again on her cheeks. 'Tracey says her jaw feels stiff,' she said.

'So does mine!' Sherie was tempted to retort, but instead she explained matter-of-factly, 'It's one of the side effects of her medication,' then added in a brighter tone to the child herself, 'Want the television on for *Sesame Street*?'

'Yes, please,' Tracey nodded hesitantly. Rapidly acquiring the experience of a veteran after several weeks on the ward, the child could sense Alison's defensive tension.

'Let's grab a quick coffee in the ward conference room,' Sherie suggested to Alison. 'You're not due off for lunch yet, are you?'

'No, I'm in the second slot today,' she replied.

Sherie took the student nurse's bare elbow in a gentle guiding grip and propelled her back down the corridor, while inwardly waiting for the outburst that told the other side of the story. It came, whispered fiercely and passionately.

'It's unethical! He treats us like slaves when we should *all* be part of a team, a medical team, skilled professionals with the common goal of...'

'I know, but Alison, you do have to be careful not to get in the way,. You *are* only a first-year student, this is your first ward, and you've only been on it for two weeks . . .'

'I was listening—I was trying to learn. How can I do that if I have to rush off to the far end of the ward whenever a doctor comes along? And even if I was in the way when I shouldn't have been, he was unpardonably rude about it! He ought to respect the fact that we're both...'

'Part of a team—I know,' Sherie nodded, unobtrusively shepherding the girl into the ward conference room and shutting the door with a quiet click.

'Would you like some coffee?'

'Don't condescend to me, Sister Page!'

'I'm not.' She stifled a spurt of real irritation. Were all eighteen-year-olds this earnest and prickly? 'It's just that you simply can't afford to be so idealistic about hospital life...'

'You said all this to me last week!'

'Exactly. So please don't make me repeat it any more. You can't expect all medical staff to be paragons. Professor Thorpe is an exceptionally skilled surgeon, and if we find him difficult personally—which we all do—then we've simply got to swallow our pride and put up with it. Please don't answer back again, not to him nor to any other medical staff member, and please be careful not to...get under his feet, Nurse Grace.' Sherie's voice was deliberately firm as she spoke the last words.

Inside, though, there was an undercurrent of

sympathy and understanding for the slim girl's fiery dedication. She decided that it was more than just a youthful naïveté. Eventually, this girl would make an excellent nurse, but she was one of those for whom the schooling process would be a turbulent one, and it was important for her to make certain adjustments in her thinking right away.

In the middle of a difficult shift, however, after working seven days straight, and on a ward that was new for herself as well, Sherie wished that she didn't have this particular problem to handle. If she chose the wrong approach, she might alienate Alison for good, and only make the girl condemn the attitudes of senior nursing staff as well.

'Now, did you want that coffee?' she finished in a warmer tone.

'No, thanks. I've got lots to get through before my lunch break. I don't want to get behind and leave my work to others.'

Alison left the conference room, and Sherie remained behind, angry at the girl and herself. Somehow, she hadn't succeeded in making headway—seemed, in fact, to have made things worse. It was clear that Alison had judged her and found her wanting in the area of professional devotion.

'If only she knew!' Sherie thought. 'If she could have seen me when I first started, doing volunteer work on my days off.'

There was a soft tap at the door, which remained slightly ajar after Alison's departure, and Lisa Perry poked her bright fair head around it.

'Sherie?'

'Yes, sorry, do you need to see me before lunch?' Sherie roused herself from her unsatisfactory reverie.

'What's up?' asked Lisa.

'What do you do with a first-year who wants to be the Lady with the Lamp?' Sherie countered with a half-smiling grimace.

'Let her get it out of her system,' Lisa replied promptly.

'When she expects senior consultants to recognise and share the inner glow, and goes into battle against them if they don't?' Sherie countered again.

'Oh dear! Not Professor Thorpe?' Lisa's face twisted comically.

'Him today, Dr Ross last Wednesday, and Mr Marzouk the Thursday before!'

'So next week it'll probably be Dr Brent. Perhaps you'd better warn him,' said Lisa. She and Sherie got on well, and had quickly taken to adopting this drawling and mock cynical tone when thrashing over ward problems together. But Sherie hadn't heard of Dr Brent.

'New paediatric oncologist, Medical side. Started yesterday,' Lisa summarised laconically. 'But you had an afternoon shift, didn't you? That's why you haven't met yet. He's a bit of a…No, I won't prejudice your first impressions,' she finished wickedly, and the exchange ended with a laugh, teasing on one side and curious on the other, although no progress had really been made over the issue of Alison Grace.

The two nurses left the conference room together to return to the large open nurses' station that formed the centre of the fifteen-bed ward. Alison was filling in charts meticulously, under a third-year's supervision, and she avoided Sherie's eye. Lisa observed this covertly and lifted her eyebrow in Sherie's direction, but nothing was said.

Mentally, Sherie had already filed this problem in the 'long-term attention' compartment of her mind,

and frankly, she was longing to get off for her break.
She hadn't managed breakfast that morning.

The telephone rang.

'Wants the Ward Sister, unless she's gone to lunch,'
reported Stephanie Dowling, the competent but
fidgety third-year, who was sitting nearest the
instrument. Sherie held out her hand for the receiver.

'Sister Page speaking.'

'Has Lucy King been transferred over from West
Six yet?' It was a deep, smooth male voice, sounding
pre-occupied.

'Yes, she has, this morning.'

'Computer hasn't caught up. I'd like to come up and
see her in about half an hour. But first could you tell
me...?'

'Just a minute, please,' Sherie interrupted skilfully,
looking at her watch.

After twelve. She was late for her break already, and
Lisa had been most involved with Lucy King so far.
'I'll put you on to Nurse Perry. But first, could I ask
who is calling?'

The question was automatic, part of her training,
and she wasn't really thinking about it. She'd report
the name to Lisa as she handed over the phone, and it
might give her a rough idea of what the caller's
question might be.

'Richard Brent, paediatric oncologist.'

Sherie's whole world suddenly lurched sickeningly
at the sound of the name. The receiver dangled limply
from her hand until Lisa took it and spoke into it.

'Hullo?'

'You look tired, Sherie,' Stephanie Dowling said,
'You won't have time to go for a proper meal. Why
don't you go?'

'Yes, I will.' Sherie summoned the faintest of

smiles, picked up a pen and put it down again, then stood up.

'Back at twelve-forty-five?' asked Lisa quickly, putting a hand over the mouthpiece of the phone she was still holding.

Sherie nodded and smiled automatically again, then got herself away, aware that several frowning faces watched her go. She walked with footsteps that snapped briskly on the impeccably polished vinyl tiles of the corridor, wanting only to get away, now, to the temporary haven of lunch. Then, on an impulse, she stopped and let herself in to the small bathroom just near the lifts.

Its quiet was disturbed only by the faint hum of air-conditioning and the occasional drip of the basin tap. Not many people noticed this room. Its door was anonymous, painted the same beige as the corridor walls and ceiling, and only discreetly marked. Most visitors tended to use the larger rooms on the ground floor, and medical staff had their own facilities in different areas. She could count fairly confidently on five minutes alone here.

The fluorescent-lit mirror exaggerated the way the colour had drained from her face, and her deep blue eyes were troubled. With fingers that almost trembled, Sherie turned the cold tap on hard and let a stream of water gush on to her up-turned palms. Then she pulled down a new length of linen from the towel dispenser and dried her hands thoroughly, taking comfort in the mechanical nature of the action.

Dr Richard Brent. There had been a time several years ago, when she first started work on the wards as a student nurse, when she had listened for that name every day, and had looked for it on every patient's card and every hospital bulletin board.

That degree of obsession had not lasted, of course, but until very recently, she had still sometimes surprised herself by feeling a thrill of dread whenever she was introduced for the first time to a group of visiting doctors. She looked at each face with trepidation, and when, one other time in the course of her career, she had come across a Dr Brent, she had felt quite sick with apprehension until she had ascertained that he was blond and named Peter.

It was only quite lately that she had stopped thinking it would ever happen. Perhaps he was a specialist in another city, or a GP in a country town, perhaps he had failed his final exams and was no longer involved in medicine at all. Statistically, the odds were high against their ever meeting again.

And now, just as that belief had thoroughly lulled her, he had turned up. Not just as a GP in a referral letter, or as a friend of a friend introduced in passing at a hospital social gathering, either, but as a permanent staff specialist who would have patient after patient on her own ward.

'I'll change wards again,' was her first thought, as she remained standing numbly in the quiet bathroom, but she dismissed the idea at once. She had applied for East Six four months ago, and it was where she wanted to be. Ward Sisters did not chop and change like that, especially if they weren't prepared to offer a reason for it, which she certainly wasn't.

'And I can't stay in here forever, either!' She spoke the words aloud in a mocking drawl, making a wry grimace at her reflection. It grimaced back. Comforting, somehow. Talking to yourself carried the stigma of being not quite healthy, but it had helped Sherie over a good few hurdles in her life—pep talks delivered in encouraging or angry tones, reasoned listing of pros and cons, and humorous quips or comments.

She thought of some of those times—the brief, doomed relationship with Mark last winter, the forced postponement of her nursing course the year after she left school, and the whole long agony of seven years ago…

Which brought things back to Richard Brent again, and the fact that she really *couldn't* stay here forever. Someone was bound to come in eventually, and besides, it wasn't quite the place for a reclusive retreat. Squaring her shoulders and swallowing her pain, Sherie reached out a steady hand to the door and pulled it open.

She ate a solitary lunch of salad sandwich, fruit and yoghurt, hiding in a distant corner of the main cafeteria where it was unlikely that any friends would see her and sit down for a chat. Chewing and swallowing were mechanical action, and when her red plastic tray was empty, she looked down at it in surprise. Had those circular thoughts absorbed her so completely that she hadn't even noticed what she was eating? Evidently.

The lift back up to the sixth floor was one of four, but it was crowded with hospital staff returning from lunch or continuing duties that took them all over the large hospital. It wasn't surprising that there should be a strange doctor amongst them, but Sherie kept hearing Richard Brent's words over the phone: 'I'll be up in half an hour.' Was it him? He had his back to her, so she couldn't be certain, and had only a glimpse of a strong hand pressing the '6' button, and wavy dark hair above broad shoulders that were clad in the classic white coat.

An electronic bell pinged out its signal that the lift was arriving, and a second later the steel doors slid

smoothly open. Sherie and the strange doctor were the
only ones to get out. Alison Grace was waiting there.
She stepped aside for Sherie and the stranger, then her
head lifted and she grinned with pleasure at the sight
of the white-coated figure.

She had not yet noticed Sherie, who decided that
perhaps she could simply slip back to the ward…Too
late!

'Oh Sister Page!, Hang on…' Alison flapped a
slender-fingered hand nervously, and giggled. 'I don't
know what to do…um…Richard…'

'Alison . . . I wondered when we'd run into each
other,' the man answered.

'I'm on one of your wards! Isn't that a coincidence?'
Excitement had raised the pitch of her voice to a
teenage squeak that was nevertheless puppy-like and
pleasant on the ear.

'Really? Which one?' He seemed almost as pleased
as she was, although his deep voice contained a note
of reserve which was probably habitual.

Both of them seemed to have forgotten Sherie, after
Alison's first awkward words. She stared at the wall,
wondering if she could edge away after all. She hadn't
dared to look the man in the face yet, but obviously it
must be Richard Brent.

'East Six. It's so interesting,' Alison was saying.
'Difficult, of course, but I'm learning a lot. You just
rang there, didn't you, and said that you were coming
up?'

'Yes, I did, and I'd better get going.' It *was* Richard.
Sherie lifted her eyes to his face. Her cheeks were
burning and she felt quite sick. He was frowning, his
dark brows drawn together.

She studied him as Alison blurted earnestly, 'Oh, of
course—you must be incredibly busy. I shouldn't

have kept you. Sorry.'

'That's all right, kitten.' The frown had gone instantly, to be replaced by a cool, blue-eyed smile, and he flicked a finger lightly against Alison's cheek as he spoke. He took a step forward, but then the eager girl stopped him again with a fluttery awkwardness that suited the endearment he had just bestowed on her.

'But oh, I must introduce you to Sister Page.' She turned quickly to Sherie, who had been trying to dissolve into the floor, her head drumming with confused disbelief and apprehension. 'Sister Page?'

'Yes, Alison?' Sherie faced the pair, outwardly calm.

'You haven't met Dr Brent yet, have you? Richard, this is Sherie Page, Ward Sister on East Six.'

'Pleased to meet you…' Sherie hesitated absurdly, her voice held on an unnatural pitch, wanting to add the all-important word 'again', but failing to bring it out, so that she finished thinly with his name: 'Dr Brent.'

'Yes, I'll look forward to working with you.' It was a conventionally polite response. Had he picked up the strained rhythm of her words? The indicators pinged again. 'Here's your lift, Allie.'

'Oh, yes—thanks. Bye, Richard.' After one last radiant smile, Alison squeezed in beside an empty meal trolley and several staff in miscellaneous uniforms. The door slid shut with a smooth clack.

Alison had a crush on Richard Brent—the fact was heart-rendingly obvious, but Sherie doubted that Alison would realise that. Did Richard? With a spurt of old, well-worn bitterness, Sherie found herself thinking that if he *did* realise it, he was quite capable of taking advantage of it.

Heaven only knew how the two of them had met;

specialists and first-year students didn't fraternise at all. But perhaps it had been in some pub or eatery near the hospital when they had both been dressed in civvies; there were a few quite good ones frequented by hospital staff in the area.

It wasn't hard to see where Alison's attractions would lie. Her pretty, lively face and manner, her eagerness, her quality of kittenish or coltish clumsiness—'Kitten', Richard Brent himself had used the word.

'On your way back to the ward?' he said casually to Sherie, breaking into her train of thought.

'Yes, I am.' Sherie fell into step beside him. What else could she do? Her heart was thudding, and it seemed incredible to her that he was clearly so relaxed. It couldn't be possible that he had failed to recognise her! Her name at the very least. It wasn't a common one.

Yet she would never have recognised Richard Brent if she had not heard his name first. His hair—much shorter now—had darkened a little to a deep brown, and the full moustache was gone, to leave him clean-shaven. He wore contact lenses instead of wire-framed John Lennon-style glasses, and she thought that perhaps it was this that made his face seem leaner, and made up of firmer planes.

His eyes were still blue, of course—a smouldering smoky blue, and that nose…Her friend and travelling companion, Robyn, had uttered an eighteen-year-old shriek when Sherie had made her eighteen-year-old confession that is was his nose that made her knees go weak. It was much the same as any other nose, straight, almost downward tilting, perhaps, but somehow so very kissable.

But it was eight long years ago that she had thought

and felt that, and mercifully the memory was very hazy after all the deliberate blocking she had done. Was his nose the same? She thought so, and of course it had to be, but she didn't have a very good visual memory when it came to the details of peoples' faces.

In summary, the changes in him were all quite natural, but they added up to more than Sherie had been expecting. She didn't know if that made this encounter better or worse. She tried to fit the face she had just studied to the never-to-be-forgotten last words he had spoken to her eight years ago—'Of course I'll ring. Two weeks from now, when I get back to Sydney. Trust me, darling, trust me.'

It didn't work.

She tried to conjure the old face in her memory, but she couldn't do that either. She had never had a photo of him; Robyn's slides hadn't come out. She had jammed a mechanism in the camera borrowed from her father and he had been furious, Sherie remembered.

'…on the phone earlier?'

'I'm sorry…' Sherie stammered. Appalled, she realised he had been speaking to her and she hadn't heard a word of it.

'I was asking if you were the nurse I spoke to on the phone before lunch.' Again it was reasoned and neutral, although he must have thought it odd, if not rude, that she had not been listening.

'No, that was Lisa Perry,' she managed. 'At least, I put you on to her halfway through.'

'That's right,' he nodded, then was silent.

She risked a glance at him and saw his eyes flick away. How long had he been studying her? He *must* know who she was.

Sherie knew that she had not changed much

physically in eight years. Her hair was longer, and she wore it off her face and neck for nursing, but the neat French plait that swept back from her high smooth forehead was as thick and straight and glossy as it had ever been. Her lips were the same wide full bow of healthy pink, her face the same well-proportioned combination of planes—high cheekbones, smooth, defined chin and jaw-line, and straight nose.

Her neck was as slender, her eyes the same blue—although they contained a depth now, revealed a capacity to suffer, that had not been there in the naïve eighteen-year-old girl she had once been. The curves of her breasts and hips were a little fuller now, perhaps. And that was the complete catalogue.

The emotional changes that had occurred would have taken longer to enumerate...

Was that smooth, neutral manner, tinged with the polite friendliness of a man meeting a junior colleague for the first time, all a pretence? Would she...was she capable of...pretending the same thing? Did she want to let him off the hook like that?

But before she had time to wonder any further about any of this, they had arrived at the ward.

CHAPTER TWO

THE two paediatric oncology wards at Prince William Hospital were very far from being the heart-breaking places that many people conjured in their minds. Sherie's ward, East Six, dealt largely with the medical side of cancer treatment, looking after children who were undergoing radiotherapy and drug therapy. Usually used in combination with surgery, these two approaches to children's cancer had dramatically improved the long-term outlook for patients in recent years, and the success rate was increasing all the time. With some forms of the disease, long-term remission was now occurring in eighty-five to ninety per cent of cases.

Of course it was not like waving a magic wand, not yet the 'miracle cure' that sensational newspapers were always claiming on medical science's behalf. Many of the children now under Sherie's care had been in and out of hospital over a period of months or even years, and for that very reason, special efforts had been made to create as warm and supportive an atmosphere as possible.

There was an activities room, there were murals on the walls, toys and books galore, and most importantly, three small rooms where parents could stay overnight, to be in constant reach and contact with their children.

Volunteers came regularly to talk and play with children, or to help them with the schoolwork that they did under the overall supervision of a trained teacher who planned lesson packages for all the children at the hospital.

There was an unspoken awareness, too, in the staffing section of the hospital that nurses assigned to this ward should have a proven record of sensitivity and empathy. Sherie had been quite proud to be taken on here as Ward Sister, after her previous experience with adult cancer care, and all in all, she was finding it a satisfying place to be. Each day brought its small miracle, and those miracles added up to counteract the effect of the inevitable tragedies that did occur now and then.

'Tran Van Thong is having his first actual radiotherapy session tomorrow, so it's just the usual dummy run today, is that right?' asked Lisa, coming up to Sherie as soon as she appeared at the nurses' section. Dr Brent had already vanished down the corridor in the direction of Bed Two.

'Yes, at two-thirty,' Sherie nodded. 'Both his parents will be there.'

'Dr Brent thought we should book an interpreter.'

'Did he?' Sherie frowned, swallowing back the inner turbulence she felt at the sound of that name. 'Their English has seemed quite adequate till now.'

'I know,' Lisa shrugged. 'But he seems to think it's necessary.'

'It's short notice for a booking,' Sherie said.

'I've rung the service and asked. They're going to call back to let me know, so cross your fingers. Dr Brent said it should have been done first thing this morning.' Lisa winced.

'What time did you try for?' asked Sherie, keeping her voice calm.

'Quarter past two,' Lisa replied. 'To meet the Van Thongs here and go down to Radio with them. Dr

Brent's going down too, and I daresay he might want you.'

'Fine,' Sherie nodded, not thinking it was fine at all. The last thing she wanted today was to be standing around with him in the radiotherapy unit, making small talk and liaising with the other staff, particularly if they'd had no success in getting an interpreter.

The phone rang and Lisa picked it up straight away, holding up her crossed fingers to Sherie. 'Yes, yes, we did,' she said in to the instrument. 'A quarter past two. You can? Terrific!'

She hung up the phone and fanned herself in mock relief. 'Let off the hook! Now I'm off to lunch.'

'Yes, go on, you're late,' answered Sherie absently.

She began some paper-work, but her concentration did not focus easily this afternoon, and she found that she was looking up far too frequently as figures passed to and fro in the area of the nurses' station.

Once it was Dr Brent who was passing, on his way out of the ward to finish some other business before he was due to return at a quarter past two. He saw the lift of Sherie's dark head, and smiled at her, forcing her to smile back, though after he had gone, the expression froze on her face and became a grimace instead.

'I don't believe it,' she thought, as the muscles in her cheeks finally relaxed again, leaving smooth planes of pale colour. 'What game is he playing?'

But what had she expected him to do? Leap back in horror and guilt? Murmur some cryptic reference to that time in their past that only she would hear? How naïve! Any man in his position would do exactly as he had done—be smoothly and casually polite until eventually the whole thing was permanently glossed over. The question was, whether Sherie was going to let him get away with that...And as yet she simply didn't know.

Alison Grace had returned from lunch now, and Sherie was at once aware of the first-year student's restlessness as she moved around the ward. The bright red head turned to look down the corridor each time someone came on to the ward—the dietician, a parent, an orderly—and then turned away again in disappointment when she saw who the arrival was.

'Um—Sister Page?' Alison had wandered up to Sherie's desk now, and was hovering about.

'Yes, Alison?' Once again Sherie paused in her work. She'd be late finishing at this rate.

A strand of bright russet hair was poked behind one ear as Alison screwed up her face a little and spoke. 'I was wondering if there'd be time for me to go down to Radio with Tran, just to see what it's like. I feel if I'm dealing with children who are having that treatment...When they're nervous about it...but if we're too busy, or if I'd be in the way...' Her clean pink nails scatched on the desk top as she fiddled with a paper clip and finished her speech.

'That sounds fine, Alison,' nodded Sherie. It would make things a little tight on the ward, but Stephanie, Melissa and Lisa could cope, and remembering the scene with Alison just before lunch, Sherie decided this was a good opportunity to start smoothing things over.

'Thank you, Sister,' Alison beamed brightly. 'That's great!'

And it was at that moment that Richard Brent returned to the ward, charcoal grey leather shoes padding rhythmically beneath charcoal grey trousers and a paler grey shirt. He was carrying his white coat. The fine material of the shirt could not altogether hide the darkness of hair on his chest beneath, nor could it blur the outlines of his firmly-sculpted shoulder muscles. Several tendrils of hair curled at this collar level, and Sherie had a sudden flash of reluctant memory—threading her fingers through Richard's hair and caressing his warm neck with her cheek and lips, eight years ago in New Zealand.

Alison's cheeks were pink immediately, and Sherie saw that his lean form in its relaxed yet good quality attire had drawn her eager gaze. With a sudden flash of suspicion, she thought, 'I wonder if I've been wrong. Perhaps Alison isn't interested in nursing at all. Perhaps this is all just designed to bring her closer to Richard.'

'Are the Van Thongs here yet?' he asked at that moment. He had come straight to Sherie's desk.

No introductory greeting or smile this time, she noticed. She met him in the eye and found that his face was masked with a very cool and very professional expression.

'Mrs Van Thong is, Mr Van Thong isn't,' she replied crisply to his question. 'He was coming straight from work, apparently.' The couple, originally refugees from Vietnam, were involved in a family furniture business.

'And the interpreter? She's been booked?'

'Actually, we've always managed to get things across in the past, so I don't know that it was necessary, but she...'

She caught his instant frown and was about to continue quickly with an assurance that Mrs Minh had been booked nonetheless, when there was a loud crash only a few yards away in the doorway of one of the four-bed sections of the ward, half-drowning her last three words.

As a reflex action, all eyes turned towards the scene, and Sherie was dismayed to see her second-year student on this shift, Melissa Thomas, standing surrounded by a litter of scattered trays and broken instruments. Melissa was intelligent, compassionate and capable, but not very adept physically, and hated her own clumsiness, so this accident would disturb her more than almost any other nursing difficulty.

'Go and help, Alison,' Sherie said quickly. A pale liquid—she hated to think what it was—was already beginning to trickle over the vinyl tiles of the floor, and slivers of glass were scattered over a radius of metres. 'Try and list everything that's broken so we can put in for replacements, and if there were any drugs on that trolley, make sure they're disposed of properly. Be super careful about broken glass too, because you know the kids trot around barefoot when they're not supposed to. Tell the four in that room to stay put until it's all cleared up.'

'OK, Sherie,' the girl nodded, and went off with alacrity, though she had glanced quickly at Richard Brent. Did she want to make sure he had noticed her willingness to work?

If she did, then she wouldn't be very satisfied, because he already seemed to have distanced himself from what was going on around the crisis site, and was wrapped in his own thoughts.

'But what business is it of mine?' Sherie thought in dismay. 'I like Alison, for heaven's sake, in spite of everything. I shouldn't be having bitchy thoughts about her like this! And as for how I feel about Richard Brent, now after so long...' But there was no time to question her feelings any further now.

'Dr Brent, isn't it? I'm so glad I caught you.' It was Mrs Maxwell, the mother of a little girl named Cindy, who was in and out of this ward, and she had some questions about care for her daughter at home. Was there a different ointment they could try to treat the dry skin that was a side-effect of her radiotherapy? And there were some diet items she'd like to ask about, too.

The paediatric oncologist responded courteously, walking with the small dark mother down the corridor towards Cindy's room as they spoke together. Sherie saw that, while her own concentration had been focused on Melissa's accident, he had put on the white coat he had been carrying. Now, he had thrust his hands into its pockets, in a position that gave him the classic silhouette of a medical man absorbed in his work.

Mr Van Thong appeared, with his usual quietly anxious frown, and Sherie realised that she had never finished her answer to Dr Brown's question about the interpreter. She *had* been booked, but no, she wasn't here yet. In fact, she was now late.

'Your wife is in with Tran now,' Sherie said to Mr Van Thong. He nodded and stood for a moment as if there was something on his mind, then went a little hesitantly in the direction of his son's room.

Sherie reached for the phone and dialled a number.

'Interpreting Service? Hi, this is Sister Page from East Six, Prince William. We booked a Vietnamese interpreter for two-fifteen—I'm afraid it was at short notice—but she hasn't arrived yet, and I was wondering...'

'Sorry, Sister, I should have rung earlier,' came a harassed female voice through the line. 'There's just been an emergency admission, a restaurant fire in Marrickville, four casualties, all Vietnamese with very little English. It's very complicated, and Mrs Minh

ly be tied up for some time. I doubt if she'll
he rest of the afternoon. Can you manage?'
'Yes, we'll be fine,' said Sherie. 'I've had no
problems with the Van Thongs in the past, and I'm a
bit surprised that Dr Brent wanted her booked in the
first place.'

'That's a relief, then,' said the Service co-ordinator.
'Now I've just got to get on the phone to Forster and
tell them why the Turkish interpreter can't make it.'

'I see, Bad day, huh?' Sherie said sympathetically,
and a groan came down the line.

'Patient for Radio? Van Thong?' said a beefy
red-faced orderly from across the desk top as soon as
Sherie had replaced the receiver.

'Oh—yes. We're not quite ready.' She glanced at
her watch. Almost half-past two, no Dr Brent, no Van
Thongs, and the small ten-year-old was due hundreds
of yards of corridor and several floors away in only a
few minutes. Schedules were tight in radiotherapy too.

Oh, but here were the Van Thongs back again.

'Bed fourteen, a little Vietnamese boy,' Sherie said
to the orderly. 'Just bring him out here, will you?'

'How is Tran? I've barely said hullo to him today,'
she said to the boy's parents.

Mr Van Thong only nodded, while his wife said,
'Good, he is good,' in a soft, heavily-accented voice.

'We're going to explain to you what will be
happening. You'll see all the equipment, and then
you'll be able to watch from behind glass,' Sherie told
them. 'You'll see what I mean when you get down
there. It's all very complicated-looking, but there's
nothing to worry about, and today is only a trial run.'

'Yes, that's good,' said Mrs Van Thong, nodding
again as her husband did. Sherie felt a sudden qualm.

'Did you understand all that? Was I speaking too

fast?'

Mr Van Thong frowned, while his wife nodded and smiled again.

'Understand. It's good.'

'Mr and Mrs Van Thong!' It was Richard Brent, and behind him after a few moments came small Tran in a wheel-chair, chauffeured by the large red hands of the orderly. 'We're running a bit late, I'm afraid…'He spoke slowly and carefully, giving added emphasis to the more difficult words. 'I was going to talk things over with you first. There should be an interpreter to help us…' He looked enquiringly at Sherie, and she shook her head, then took in a breath to explain the situation. Before she could speak, though, she saw his jaw set in anger and he turned to the Van Thongs again.

'Well, it seems I was wrong. We'll just have to manage. I'll explain a little as we go, and then I'll leave you with the radiotherapy staff and they'll tell you the rest. We won't need you to come with us, Sister Page.'

'They've understood everything up till now,' Sherie put in quickly as an aside to the paediatric oncologist, '—or said they did,' she added in sudden doubt, as he turned impatiently away.

The small procession of Tran, his parents, the orderly and Dr Brent departed, without the latter having replied to her last words, and she watched him go, biting her lip.

He was clearly angry, and his anger was directed at her, which was grossly unfair. He hadn't given her half a chance to explain about the emergency admissions from the restaurant fire. Angry herself now, she turned back to the paperwork she had now been away from for some minutes, her glance connecting with Alison Grace's for a moment.

The younger nurse was still involved in clearing up

the trolley disaster with Melissa, but it was obvious that she had seen and heard the recent brief exchange, and from her expression it was clear that she thought Dr Brent was in the right.

Sherie felt an absurd impulse to gabble out an explanation to the girl, but stifled it quickly. She certainly didn't want to get into the habit of justifying her actions and decisions to an over-critical and starry-eyed junior, especially when it appeared as if that junior had some kind of acquaintanceship outside the hospital with the man Sherie had once loved…the man who had devastated her life.

Only then did Sherie remember that she had given permission for Alison to go down to radiotherapy with the Van Thongs and Dr Brent.

'Oh, Alison, I'm sorry,' Sherie said immediately, contrite. It was too late for her to go now.

'It's all right.' Alison drew herself up haughtily, wary of expressing her disappointment.

'No, it isn't. I forgot you, so you've missed out. There'll be another chance, so please remind me next time Dr Brent is taking someone down,' Sherie said apologetically.

'Yes, OK, then, thank you, Sister,' the girl nodded stiffly.

She seemed awkward, and Sherie wondered if she felt she had betrayed too openly her feelings about Richard Brent. Well, she had. Crushes were difficult things to disguise when you were eighteen. As you got older, it became easier to mask one's feelings…Or did it?

Impatiently she shook off this unproductive train of thought, and turned back to her work. What was the time? Ten to three. The incoming shift would be arriving any minute now.

'Excuse me, could you help me, please?' The interruption came half an hour later. The shift change-over, with it's short conference between those coming on and those going off, had already come and gone, but Sherie could not leave until she had completed this paperwork . . .

She looked up, masking her reluctance, and encountered the eager stare of a middle-aged woman with large bones and rather prominent white teeth and green eyes. She wore the pink floral uniform and plastic name-badge of the hospital volunteer service, and she carried an armful of children's books.

'You've come to read to the children?' asked Sherie.

'Oh!' The woman seemed taken aback. 'Well, I've brought these books. I didn't know I was supposed to read to them. This is my first day. I think I'm supposed to go back and find out my next little job straight away.'

'Of course, that's fine, You can just leave the books here, and someone will take them to the activities room in a minute'.

The woman did as Sherie had suggested, dumping the books on the bench, then leaned confidentially towards her. 'This is the ward where all the poor little children are dying, isn't it?'

Sherie bristled instantly at the ghoulish question. 'They certainly are not!' she said crisply.

'Oh, but I thought…This is the cancer ward, isn't it?'

'Yes, it is, but that does *not* mean that every patient we have here is dying!' Sherie spoke quietly, in case there were any parents around who could well be deeply angered and upset by the mistaken assumption.

'It's incurable, though, I mean, they haven't found a cure yet…' the woman was continuing. Judy Colton,

Ward Sister on the afternoon shift, was on the phone nearby, and Sherie suspected that she was listening to this conversation with half an ear.

'That's not quite true, Mrs Beasley,' said Sherie, glancing quickly at the woman's name-badge. 'Our success rate is very high indeed. If you'd like to read a bit more about it, I can give you some pamphlets...'

'Oh, no, not today. Another time, perhaps. I'd better get back to HQ.' She chuckled at her mild joke, and just at that moment, Sherie saw Richard Brent's tall figure looming behind the woman.

'All right, then. Perhaps we'll see you again,' she said. The paediatric oncologist was clearly waiting to speak to her, and she wondered how long he would be prepared to stand in line behind the worst kind of hospital volunteer. Judy was off the phone now. She looked questioningly at Dr Brent, but he shook his head, so she went on with her other business, which now took her along the corridor and out of sight.

'Yes, I'm sure you will see me again.' Mrs Beasley nodded. Her smile revealed long teeth and pink gums again. 'It's very distressing, this kind of work, though isn't it? Some of the awful lives that people have! I heard about one poor woman in another ward who... But that'd be a breach of patient confidentiality if I told you about it, wouldn't it? So I'd better not.'

'No, that's right,' Sherie agreed firmly.

The woman said a cheery good-bye and left the ward, having no notion that she might have in any way given offence.

Most volunteers at the hospital were genuinely compassionate people, but this was a type that Sherie had struck before, and she found it difficult to deal with the ghoulish curiosity and sensationalism of the woman's attitude. For a moment, her hand hovered over the telephone as she thought of ringing Mrs McDonald, the full-time volunteer co-ordinator, but then she decided against it. It was already way past the end of her shift, and Mrs McDonald was perceptive about her volunteers. This one would soon be put into some safe area where there was no risk of her attitude upsetting anyone, and perhaps in time Mrs Beasley would learn some real care, and that attitude would change. In any case, Dr Brent was waiting.

'Why did you not book an interpreter as I had asked?' He had moved forward and was leaning angrily across the chest-high laminate bench-top that marked off the nurses' station.

'Lisa did book her...' Sherie stammered awkwardly, startled by his nearness—she could see the dark hair that curled on his chest where his shirt was open at the neck—and by the steely glint in his slate-blue eyes, not to mention the hard set of his jaw.

'And you cancelled her because you'd always managed to get things across before?'

'No! Don't jump to conclusions, Dr Brent.' Her own tone was icy and deliberate now.

'Have you any idea what a mess we've just been through down in Radio? Putting the whole day's schedule back? The Van Thongs became completely confused and frightened—' He stopped abruptly as a third-year nurse smiled apologetically and tiptoed around him to look up a chart.

He nodded briefly at the nurse and disguised the hard clamp of his hand on Sherie's arm so that it looked like merely a polite supporting gesture.

'Let's go into the ward conference room. I need a coffee.'

When the door had shut behind them, Sherie faced him boldly.

'You haven't given me the ghost of an opportunity to explain,' she said fiercely. 'Mrs Minh was booked for two-fifteen. When she didn't turn up, I rang the Service and it turns out there'd been four emergency admissions, and all Vietnamese and all needing her help. Put against that, the Van Thongs didn't have a claim.

'She should have been booked for two.'

'That's a meaningless quibble under the circumstances,' Sherie retorted, not bothering to point out that in any case it had been Lisa's decision. 'She couldn't have come at two either.'

What was all this about? Eight years ago in New Zealand? Would she confront him with that? No, not just now, this wasn't the time or place. With a pang of intense self-doubt, she wondered when and where she *would* have the courage to do it.

He was at the urn making two coffees, although he hadn't asked her if she wanted one. As it happened, she did, but she felt more like flinging it in his face than drinking it.

'All right,' he said after a moment, speaking with studied patience, 'We're both making meaningless quibbles.'

'And you've been accusing me of going against your instructions without even bothering to listen to my side of the story!'

'Then I apologise,' he drawled, 'But next time, don't be so eager to assure me of your good communication skills with migrant patients.'

'You're suggesting that I have an inflated view of—'

'I'm suggesting that there's often more to a situation like this than meets the eye. You haven't worked on a children's ward before?'

'No, no I haven't.' She didn't tell him the reason: that only now, after seven years, was she ready to deal with children again, only now, she found her work with them was healing her remaining pain instead of opening the wound afresh.

'Then perhaps you haven't come across the problem. Children learn a new language much faster and more easily than adults, and yet a lot of adult migrants in this country are embarrassed or afraid to admit their English isn't good—scarcely surprising, sometimes, when you hear what experiences some of them have had. The Van Thongs fall into that group.'

'I see,' Sherie said slowly.

'They pretend to understand, they nod, and smile and say, "Yes", and "Good", they can handle basic conversation quite well. "How are you", "It's a nice day, isn't it?" But for anything more complicated, they rely on Tran.'

His words were measured now. His voice deeper and more pleasantly resonant than Sherie had remembered. That happened sometimes, of course, with increased age...With a guilty start at the way her thoughts had briefly strayed, Sherie turned her attention back to his words.

'Yesterday, I was seeing the patient in the bed next to Tran, just after I'd explained something to the Van Thongs. They'd said that yes, they understood, but then I heard them turn to Tran and ask some questions in Vietnamese, which he replied to in a long and very involved and hesitant way. After they'd gone, I asked him what it was about and got the truth. They hadn't understood at all, and Tran had had to explain the whole thing from memory. You can imagine the misunderstandings that leads to! A ten-year-old, who only speaks Vietnamese at home, or perhaps a little in the playground at school, scarcely has the vocabulary to describe precise details of medical treatment.' He faced her with challenge in his eyes after the long speech.

'I should have guessed.' Sherie's anger had gone now that she had got caught up in this very human story. She had to admire his perception. 'So, how did you manage today?'

'With a lot of pointing and gesturing and a lot of hard work for poor Tran. It's not particularly satisfactory for a ten-year-old to have to explain his own treatment to his parents, especially when it's something like radiotherapy, but if we hadn't spent the time and effort, the parents would have gone away more anxious than when they arrived, and we might have had trouble getting their consent to the treatment.'

'I'll be more aware in future,' Sherie nodded.

'I'm sure you will be,' was his clipped reply.

There was an awkward silence, broken suddenly by the insistent electronic piping of a paging device from Richard Brent's pocket. He took it out, pressed a red button on top and spoke into it briefly, his expression betraying relief at the interruption.

'That'll be Dr Martin on West Six—I was expecting it. I'll see you again soon, no doubt, Sister Page.'

He left at once, and two cups of coffee stood cooling down on the draining board beside the urn, Sherie tipped them both down the sink, feeling suddenly tired to the marrow of her bones. Richard Brent, after all these years, and to have to relate to each other like this, as specialist and Ward Sister...

In five minutes, she had left East Six and was on her way home. When she reached her small Toyota and opened the door, she was greeted by a wave of suffocating air. It was a scorching hot day—especially in contrast to the air-conditioned hospital building—although it was only late November. The car had been parked in the sun since early that morning; it's vinyl seat would literally burn her thighs.

Wearily, she stretched an arm over the seat-back, picked up an old towel from the floor and spread it out on the seat, then eased herself in. The gear stick and steering-wheel were almost too hot to touch, too. Half an hour of traffic to negotiate before she reached the breezy haven of the old-fashioned but very comfortable Kirribilli flat she shared with Robyn.

Would Robyn be home? Probably. Her hours at North Shore Childrens' Hospital were the same as Sherie's today. And would Sherie mention Richard Brent? She felt sick at the thought of having to put it all into words. No, she wouldn't say anything.

But then she thought of how long they had been friends, and what they had helped each other through, how honest they had always been with each other, and how loyal. Robyn would have to know.

CHAPTER THREE

'JUST forget about it,' said Robyn, nodding her rather plain face sympathetically. 'You've had a rotten day, but the medical world only has a few Professor Thorpes, after all.'

'But I haven't finished yet,' Sherie said, after a slight pause.

'Oh no! Ward Sister throws bedpan in consultant's face!' Robyn staggered dramatically towards the kitchen, one hand pressed to her forehead and the other flapping violently.

'Not quite!'

'Perhaps I'd better mix you a hook, line and sinker.'

'Oh, yes, please! But go easy on the hook part—a teaspoon of it would go to my head in this heat,' Sherie replied, sounding more lighthearted than she felt.

She put a hand to her hair, thinking of releasing it from its tight confining plait, then felt the soft curling tendrils of damp hair on her neck and changed her mind. Loose, it would only be hotter and heavier. She listened to Robyn pouring the cool drink—a modest slosh of chilled white wine, a dash of lime cordial and a fizzy fill of soda water topped with clinking ice cubes.

It wasn't hard to postpone the telling of her story. She took a long refreshing mouthful from the misted glass before she finally spoke.

'We've got a new paediatric oncologist on East Six. I met him today for the first time just after lunch.'

'Oh yes?'

The room seemed suddenly quiet and still. The jazz record Robyn had been playing had finished and the automatic player shut off with a click. Robyn had quite an eager nose for the dramatic, and she didn't make a move to turn the record over just at this point.

'Richard Brent.'

'Oh, Sherie!'

'He's changed—in looks, I mean, I wouldn't have recognised him.'

'Did he recognise you?' asked Robyn.

'If he did, he didn't say.'

'And then when he heard your name, surely…'

'By then, he'd decided not to show it, evidently.'

'He must acknowledge you next time, though,' Robyn insisted.

'Why? Eight years is a long time. It's scarcely important any more.' Sherie laughed, heard the bitterness in it and was angry with herself.

'It's important to you,' said Robyn.

'There were plenty of reasons for that, and he didn't share them.'

'That's just too right! People like that always get off lightly!' Robyn's voice was bitter now, and Sherie reacted against it.

'That's not fair,' she said. 'Mark wasn't like that. Or Paul.'

'But things didn't work out for you with them, did they?'

'That was my fault, though, not theirs. I couldn't…I just couldn't…'

'You couldn't trust them because of what happened with Richard,' Robyn finished for her, scraping her rather heat-wilted brown hair off her forehead.

'I can't let one bad experience colour my feelings for the rest of my life,' said Sherie with slow intensity.

'Plenty of people think they've fallen in love, and that its mutual, and then never hear from the person again. It's a fairly rotten thing to do, but it's not a crime, making all those promises and not keeping them...'

'But most people don't have to go through what you went through afterwards,' Robyn countered indignantly.

'Richard didn't know about any of that.'

'He should have known. If he'd rung you when he got back from Sydney, kept in contact as he said he would, then he'd have found out and he'd have been able to support you through it. Everything would have been different...'

'But would I have wanted that support if it wasn't given willingly?' Sherie said wearily. 'We'd just finished our matriculation, and he'd just finished medical school. We were all having a great old carefree time in New Zealand. If it was just a holiday romance for him, if it was just a physical attraction—and it obviously must have been—then perhaps the most honest thing to do was exactly what he did: never contact me again.'

'Why are you defending him, Sherie? What's got into you? The man has ruined your life utterly—'

'*Utterly*?' echoed Sherie. 'That's far too strong a—'

But Robyn was still quivering with righteous indignation. 'I should know, I went through it all with you. It's as if you don't *want* to be angry with him any more.' She paused for a moment, and then said in a different tone, 'You said he'd changed physically. Is he still as good-looking?'

'I suppose so.'

'Well, Sherie, your defences seem to have dropped remarkably quickly,' Robyn said significantly, 'and all I can say is...'

'Don't say anything, I'm sorry I told you.' Sherie clamped her mouth tight shut after the words and closed her eyes, their thick lashes forming two dark crescents on her angry pink cheeks.

There. Now she and Robyn were on the point of an argument. Robyn was silent, clearly hurt. Sherie groped amongst confused feelings for the right thing to say. She *was* sorry she'd told Robyn. Why? Why was she feeling so irritated? The rattly old doorbell sounded before she had found any words.

'That'll be Bernard,' said Robyn, after taking a deep breath. 'We're going to a film and then dinner in Dixon Street with a few people.' She jumped up and started for the door. 'I've still got to change, too.'

'Robyn, I…Let's not…' Sherie began, but Robyn's expression made it clear that for her the topic was closed.

Sherie summoned some bright conversation and a cool drink for the shy doctor who had been Robyn's steady boyfriend for a year now, while the latter got dressed, and then the two of them were ready to leave.

'Sure you don't want to come?' Robyn offered gruffly.

'No, thanks, I'm going to have a cold shower and tuna salad for tea, and curl up with a good book,' said Sherie. Bernard jangled his car keys and started down the steps. Sherie added quietly, 'Sorry I snapped.' The apology was still an effort.

'Sorry I nagged,' Robyn returned, also with an effort. The issue hadn't really been resolved.

'We can talk about it some more tomorrow,' Sherie said.

'Only if you want to, Shezz.' Robyn used a vintage nickname, but her tone was still stiff. 'I can tell you'd rather not. Maybe we've both been living through this for too long. After all, as you said, Richard never even knew about…' Her pause was too significant, and again Sherie felt a restless spurt of emotion that she could not name.

'About Simon,' she finished matter-of-factly.

'Have a good relaxing evening, then,' said Robyn.

'You too,'

Robyn and Bernard disappeared out of the door. Sherie poured herself a plain iced water and stood out on the balcony, in the corner of it that was shaded from the late afternoon sun. The water in the Harbour sparkled only a few hundred yards away, and the white sails of boats were increasing in number all the time as people took to the water after their day's work, for evening races or simply for harbour picnics.

Some people said that you got blasé about a view like this after a couple of months, and that you stopped noticing it, but Sherie and Robyn had been living here for two years now, and they weren't sick of it yet. It was worth putting up with the two poky bedrooms and the primitive state of the kitchen and bathroom for the sake of the sunny little lounge-room and this adjoining balcony with its matchless panorama.

Sherie's father, a widower, owned the flat, although he himself lived several suburbs away in a flat of his own. Although the two girls paid him a good rent, it was getting to be rather less than what similar places in the area were now commanding. They were lucky, and both knew it.

To the right, as Sherie looked out, was the criss-cross metal arc of the bridge, its shape distorted from this angle. Almost directly in front was the Opera House, its roof so closely echoing the outline of the yachts that tacked to and fro in front of it. And to the left was Fort Denison, its pitted sandstone walls lapped by the dark green water.

The backdrop of the modern city skyline had a different beauty, too, especially at night, and they could have sold tickets for their view of the New Year fireworks.

Sherie felt her spirits lift on the salt breeze, and her heart went over to the boats and floated with them on the rhythmic swell and fall of the water, so that she was almost freed from her thoughts for a welcome few moments. Only a few moments, though. It hadn't been a good day.

She slept badly that night, haunted by dreams, but she was beetling her small car across the Bridge punctually the next day, in the warm bright light of the early summer morning, and the thought of plunging into work again was a pleasurable one—since today wasn't due to be one of Richard Brent's days, apparently.

Sherie's step was light and quick as she walked down the corridor from the lift, and her mind was already carefully running through some of the day's projected events. She looked at her watch. Only twenty to seven. The early-bird traffic on the Harbour Bridge had been unusually light, but she had deliberately aimed to arrive before seven, feeling still that she needed to keep a step ahead on this new ward.

Engaged in poking a recalcitrant pin back into one shining curve of the neat French pleat in which she had styled her hair that morning, and wrapped in thought as she was, Sherie did not notice the open ward conference room door. Nor did she see the long figure that uncurled itself from one of the chairs within and came out to her.

'Sister Page!'

She started, turned, then went weak when she saw

that it was Richard Brent.

'I thought you didn't usually come in on Wednesdays.' It was an awkward, blurted statement, and his reply to it was blunt and seemed cool.

'I'm not "in". I came to see you.'

'Oh?'

This was it, then. Last night he had made a decision to bring their past relationship out into the open, while she was still hanging back, unable to face the scene that would follow.

'Yes, I'm on my way to an early game of tennis, as you can see,' he drawled, and gestured down at the clothing he wore.

The athletic apparel emphasised the lazy power and masculine grace of his body. Snug-fitting navy blue tracksuit pants contrasted with an utterly white short-sleeved tennis shirt, that was open at the neck to reveal dark hair. He wore tennis shoes, too, and had a grey sweat-shirt slung over his shoulders.

Sherie took it all in for the first time. Till now, in the few moments they had stood facing each other, she had been too involved in searching his face, as she had yesterday, for the expressions and features she remembered from eight years ago. Some of them were there, she thought, but then in a sudden flood of self-doubt she wondered if everything she thought she remembered of the younger Richard was simply a hazy romantic fabrication created by a starry-eyed schoolgirl.

The lazy smile which hinted at hidden emotional depth, the teasing twinkle in his eyes, the way they clouded with love… That was the way she had thought of it all then, in her naïveté. Now, of course, she could find none of it.

'I was too pessimistic about the traffic—that's why

I'm so early, if that's what you were wondering,' he added with heavy pointed patience, and she realised that she had been gawping at him for some moments.

'Sorry,' she managed to apologise, 'I was…impressed with your energy at this time of the morning, that's all. You wanted to see me. Is it all right just to sit in here? I'll make us some coffee. It's good that I came in before time or you wouldn't have caught me.'

Now she was talking too much, and it was almost worse than her silence had been. She was choosing to pretend that he had come to see her purely on ward matters, and risked a side-long glance at him as she started towards the sink area, to see if he was fooled by it, or if he would decide to play along for the moment, anyway.

But she could tell nothing from his expression. There was a faintly quizzical tilt to the angle of his well-shaped head, perhaps, but that was all, and he just stood there, feet planted slightly apart on the vinyl-tiled floor, as if he was waiting for his partner to serve a ball.

'It was the only time I could fit in for a game,' he said. He had only nodded briefly to her suggestion of coffee.

'This is dreadful!' Sherie thought, as she refuged over the coffee preparation at the kitchen unit in the far corner of the ward conference room. 'It's like an American soap opera, and I hate being one of the characters. I can't play the role at all. I want to run away, and not face some hideous confrontation.'

And yet, if there was a confrontation, it would be herself who started it, she realised. Richard had never known about Simon. Why bring up all that pain within herself by talking about it? When he said whatever he was planning to say about those weeks in New Zealand, why confront him with the fact of her pregnancy?

Why not just laugh and say that actually it had taken *her* all last night to work out why his name seemed familiar? And wasn't it funny how young love took itself so seriously, and then was so soon forgotten? Something like that…

Yes. That was quite adequate, involved no naked display of bitterness or emotion…acknowledged the past connection, but made it clear that they were now off to a fresh start.

Except that this last was not quite the truth, she admitted to herself. Yesterday, she had blamed Robyn for fanning the flame of her bitter feelings, and their coolness with one another had not yet been resolved. But it was unfair to heap everything on her. Sherie still felt far too bitter herself, too clouded with the past. Suddenly she knew that it was inevitable that she would tell Richard Brent the whole long story one day.

Perhaps not now, but another time when for some reason her guard was down. The whole thing seemed like some vicious animal lying in wait for her. She knew it was there, but the way was narrow and she could not avoid the place where the animal would spring…

'Here it is,' she said brightly to Richard Brent when she approached him with the coffee a few moments later.

'Looks good,' he said, offhand and polite.

They each helped themselves to milk and biscuits in silence. Neither took sugar, although they had both taken two spoonfuls back in the New Zealand days. Then he added, 'Although I shouldn't be eating before a game.'

'Singles or doubles?' It was pure small talk.

'Doubles, Mixed.'

'You're not the only early riser, then.'

'You play?'

'Yes,' she nodded reluctantly, as if admitting to some vice. They had played together twice in New Zealand. He had beaten her, but not by all that much. Evidently he still had not remembered their relationship in much detail.

'On the courts here at the hospital?'

'No, with some friends at a club on the North Shore,' she replied.

'You should try it here, The courts are magnificent—surrounded by trees and flowers—hibiscus, jasmine, jacaranda, wattle, bougainvillaea.'

'Yes, I must remember to bring my racquet and organise a game after work some time,' she said, wondering how long they could spin out this conversational rally.

She had a fleeting moment in which to feel surprised that he had called all those shrubs and trees so enthusiastically by name. The Richard Brent of eight years ago had not been so interested in botany or gardening, although he had known the make and model of an impressive number of top-of-the-range cars.

Still, people changed and matured. Their interests broadened and deepened. She wondered in what other ways he might have changed, wanted to study his face again, but could not bear to risk meeting the gaze from those cool blue eyes. She had been looking away from his ever since she had come over with the coffee—down at her cup and biscuit, across at a seascape print on the opposite wall.

'Is anything the matter?' His unexpectedly gentle

question forced her to look at him finally.

His voice was very deep, his delivery slow, as if he was a man who weighed his words carefully, and his Australian accent was not at all strong. In fact, at times he sounded almost English. Again, it was not what Sherie had remembered, and she wondered how and where he had spent the past eight years.

'No, I was just wondering…what you had to say to me, that's all,' she replied weakly, after a small pause.

He was sitting back in the low black fabric-covered arm-chair, his limbs lazily graceful as if they were limbered frequently on the courts. His eyes were slightly narrowed, yet they did not seem cold. Rather, he looked as if he could guess at part of what she was feeling, and had sympathy for it. Or pity. Which was the last thing she wanted, since it carried the implication that she was still hungering for him after all this time. Sherie's chin suddenly lifted defiantly and she spoke strongly, before he had time to reply.

'Because I'm pretty busy, today, I came in early to get a head start, but time's already getting on.'

'Ah, of course,' was his quiet reply. He seemed taken aback by her change of manner, yet surely he must know that she was far from spineless! What did he have to propose? That they pretend never to have met? Easy enough, and she would happily agree to it. Why didn't he get it over with?

'If you want to be businesslike,' he continued, 'then it's two things, First, I want to apologise about yesterday, I overreacted. The session with Mr and Mrs Van Thong came on top of various other problems, and then on top of *that*, when I wanted to talk to you about it, I had to wait until that ghoulish idiot of a woman in the floral uniform had finished sniffing out the gruesome details of modern paediatric cancer treatment.'

Unwillingly, Sherie laughed, and saw that his answering smile was accompanied by a narrowing of his eyes that bespoke satisfaction. He was deliberately trying to break down her defences and win her over, so he'd never have to risk her making a scene. Was that it?

'Secondly,' Richard was continuing, 'I like to get to know my senior nursing staff properly—and everyone I work with, eventually—and I don't think we should rely on that happening purely over ward reports and accounts. We had a rather unsatisfactory first meeting yesterday. I don't want that to set the tone for our whole relationship. I had half an hour to fill in before the game, so I thought this was a good way to make use of it.'

He finished the explanation with another disarming smile that made Sherie freeze further. He was definitely looking at her curiously.

'What in particular did you want to find out about me?' she enquired sweetly, lifting her head again. She knew that her cheeks were a little pink, and had been told in the past that this was part of her beauty, highlighting and giving added life to her blemish-free skin and to the darkly contrasting mass of braided hair.

But she might have preferred to look sallow and frumpish this morning. It had only ever been her looks that had attracted him eight years ago. He had spent all his time wooing her physically, had never even known what lay beneath.

He took in a breath to reply, then appeared to change his mind, and paused for a judicious few seconds.

'Perhaps you'd like to tell me about your attitude towards parental presence during drug therapy for children with Ewing's Sarcoma,' he said deliberately after the pause had grown uncomfortably long.

Sherie's jaw dropped and she struggled.

'It depends on the…If the child…I think different cases call for different decisions, but we have no Ewing's Sarcoma on East Six at the moment. Is someone being admitted? I don't understand…' She finally trailed to a halt, then stiffened as she saw the rather malicious smile that played around his mouth but did not reach his eyes.

'Sister Page, you must realize that what I had in mind can't be gleaned by questions fired at you like at a job interview!' he said impatiently. 'For heaven's sake! I felt like a coffee and I thought we could sit and talk. You play tennis. What else do you do? Let's find out something about each other.'

Sherie still sat stiffly, 'I know quite a lot about you already,' she could have said, but didn't. Instead she answered his question blandly, knowing that what she said would tell him nothing of importance.

'I like gardening, cooking, reading, films, dance. What about you? What have you been doing since you finished your training?'

'Since I finished my training? That long ago?'

'Well, I meant…' She had slipped a little, had unconsciously been asking for a run-down on the past eight years of his life. 'Have you had time for outside interests? When did you decide to specialise in this area?'

A knock at the door startled them both and saved her from having to listen to his reply to her stilted questions. As if Richard Brent knew that it would be a permanent interruption to their awkward and unsuccessful talk, he quickly drained the last half of his coffee and stood up, while Sherie cleared a slightly husky throat to call, 'Come in!'

Then she stood up as well.

It was Alison Grace who opened the door, her bright strawberry-blonde head bobbing gracefully as she spoke.

'Sorry, Sister Page, I wanted to...Oh!' She broke off sharply as she caught sight of Richard Brent's tall, capable form, and her face was flooded with what was clearly, to Sherie, envy. 'I didn't realise you had someone important with you—I'll see you about it later.'

'It doesn't matter, Allie, I'm about to go.' Richard said roughly, with more than a hint of anger and impatience.

Alison flinched and stared down quickly, clearly hurt by his tone. She was far too sensitive, Sherie reflected. She wouldn't survive life as a nurse if she didn't develop a tougher hide and more emotional control. The whole ward would know about her crush on Richard Brent soon.

The paediatric oncologist was obviously aware of the tension in the atmosphere of the small room, and he seemed oppressed and irritated by it. His tennis shoes raked dully on the carpet square in the middle of the floor as he shifted his weight and turned to Sherie.

'We'll try this another time—perhaps coffee at seven in the morning wasn't the best idea. I'm sure I'll catch you over a break during the week. I must get down to the court.'

He reached across in front of Sherie to snatch up the grey sweatshirt from the small desk where he had flung it earlier, and she caught the sudden scent of his aftershave, mingled with a faint tang of clean, healthy maleness. An unmistakable flood of awareness rose in her, and was disturbing.

She took in a sharp breath. It was soundless, thank goodness, but she saw that Alison had given her a quick glance. Had she noticed something?

It seemed that Richard Brent had not. He tipped a quick wink at the eager young girl as she stepped aside for him to pass through the door, and then he was gone, the rubber soles of his shoes squeaking on the vinyl tiles in an athletic rhythm. Alison listened to the sound until it died away, the glow gradually fading from her cheeks and eyes as she did so.

'Did you want to talk to me in here?' Sherie asked with an effort. An echo of the surge that had passed through her moments ago still remained, and she was horrified by it. Was her body still susceptible to him after all this time?

'Yes, here would be fine,' Alison was saying. 'It won't take long. I just wanted to say that I've thought about what you said to me yesterday about Professor Thorpe and all that, and I don't think you're right. I'm not trying to be insubordinate or anything, but I just thought you ought to know.'

Sherie stifled a sigh and nodded slowly.

'Actually, I thought I might talk to Richard about it and see what he says.' Alison's finely-modelled jaw lifted slightly, and Sherie nodded again.

'Yes, that's probably a good idea,' she said evenly. 'Everyone has a different perspective on hospital life.'

'I hope you're not angry?'

'No, I'm not,' She *was* wearied by the whole thing, though, as she foresaw an even longer period of turmoil and adjustment for Alison than she had initially imagined.

'Well, that's good,' Alison nodded, brightly and politely, 'Shall I go on to the ward now?'

'Yes, go along, I'll be there in a minute myself.'

Alison left, her movements neat and lithe in her pale blue uniform. Sherie watched her for a moment, then followed. In spite of the girl's gaucheness and naïveté there was something very winning in her eagerness. Sherie could see how Richard Brent might be flattered by the adoration.

Sherie herself had been like Alison in so many ways at eighteen. Richard had been twenty-four when they had met in New Zealand, anxiously awaiting the results of his finals while touring the country on the cheap, as she and Robyn had been. So he was now…what? Thirty -two. Too old for Alison, but that wouldn't necessarily stop him seducing her.

Suddenly Sherie felt a spurting flood of intense anger and dislike that completely quenched her earlier disturbing flame of awareness. She wanted to warn Alison somehow.

'This man will use you, if you get involved with him. Perhaps he doesn't even realise it, but he will. It'll last about two weeks. Get out now, while you still can.'

But she knew that these words, or any like them, would never be spoken. Alison couldn't even listen to a mild criticism of her over-intense attitude to her work. How much less open would she be to anything that bruised a hero-worshipping infatuation with Richard Brent?

And Sherie was not exactly an impartial observer in all this.

'I'll have to confront him,' she realised, 'and soon. Or it'll fester inside me like poison.' But not yet. Not yet.

CHAPTER FOUR

'HAVE you remembered to change over your patch lately, Jonathan?'

Sherie paused at the door of the activities room where three children were involved in a game of Monopoly that was in danger of getting a little out of hand. It was five days after her encounter over morning coffee with Richard Brent, and she had had a day off, followed by three more days on afternoon shifts.

'No, I forget sometimes,' he said sheepishly, then quickly shifted the black eye patch he wore from one eye to the other, and blinked gingerly as he adjusted to the change.

Ten-year-old Cindy Maxwell and nine-year-old Paul White giggled. They were both in for regular follow-up chemotherapy after earlier radiotherapy and surgery—Cindy for a Wilms tumour, and Paul for the once-dreaded Rhabdomysarcoma. Both were approaching the second anniversary of their initial surgery, and everyone was now beginning to feel very optimistic about their chances for long-term survival and health. Jonathan's surgery had been quite minor, and he was only on this ward because West Six was temporarily full.

Richard Brent was waiting in the nurses' station as Sherie approached, after taking a jigsaw puzzle to another child. He was sitting back casually in a vinyl swivel chair, with his feet, clad in comfortable white leather shoes, resting against the green laminex edge of one of the long built-in desks.

She had not seen him since he had left for his tennis game last Wednesday, although she knew from reading notes and reports from Judy Colton and other staff that he had appeared several times during different shifts over the past few days.

When she reached him, after nodding and murmuring a brief greeting to which he responded in kind, she saw that the relaxed pose wasn't quite genuine, though. He was actually holding himself very tightly. Fleetingly, she wondered if he had changed his mind about bringing up the subject of their shared past, but then dismissed the idea. There was something in his expression which told her it was ward business.

'What's happened?' she asked. It was abrupt, but he didn't seem to care.

'I just had a run-in with a parent. Can we go somewhere private?' His tone was low and controlled as ever, giving nothing away.

In keeping with the policy of the ward, visiting hours were extensive, and as well as staff, there were one or two mothers about, although it was the middle of a Monday morning. Sherie glanced around briefly, then spoke.

'I'd rather stay here to—to keep an eye on things.'

That wasn't the real reason, of course.

'And I'd rather go somewhere private.' It was deceptively mild.

Sherie dared to meet his eyes for a moment and saw that they were steady and cold, although the frown that drew his well-drawn brows together, wasn't quite one of anger. There was something almost wary in the way he was holding himself now.

'All right, then.' It sounded reluctant and

ungracious, and Sherie amended the error quickly, adding in a brighter tone, 'The ward conference room would be best, I expect, wouldn't it? In case either of us is needed.'

'If that's what you'd prefer.' His penetrating eyes were still regarding her steadily, and for a moment she almost thought he had guessed that her reason for choosing that room was more because it was large—enabling her to put more distance between them—than because it was near the nucleus of ward activity.

She thought about suggesting coffee, then decided against it. Why turn this into a semi-social occasion, when she wanted to keep it utterly businesslike? Then she felt angry at herself. She should either say something to him about their shared past, or put it behind her, not let the whole thing drag on like this.

But Richard made straight for the urn and coffee bench in the corner of the room, in any case, held up a cup to her questioningly, then, after her head-shake, made a strong one for himself.

She waited until he had sat down, fiddling with something at the opposite end of the room to make an excuse for remaining on her feet, then took a seat several feet distant from him. He had not leant back in his seat but was sitting with elbows on knees, drawing in long gulps of his steaming drink.

'Ken Williams has just spent an hour in my office,' he said after he had nearly emptied the cup.

Sherie nodded slowly and silently, beginning to have an inkling of what was coming. She waited for Dr Brent to continue, but for a good while he did not. Instead, he drained the last of his coffee and then sat back at last, and when he put his cup down, Sherie saw that his hand—lean, sinewy and tanned—shook slightly.

'He's had a lot of trouble accepting Robert's illness,' she put in now, realising—and finding it surprising—that the paediatric oncologist's words were not coming easily.

'Robert is only five years old, and he won't reach his next birthday. I don't blame his parents for…but it's been a pretty gruelling session, and I don't know that anything has been resolved. I wanted to warn you about it because Mr Williams is coming here in his lunch break…'

'Yes, he often does that,' Sherie interjected, thinking of how difficult those visits sometimes were.

'…And you may get some pretty nasty threats.'

'Threats?'

'Legal action, a media scandal, violence…'

'Oh, Richard!' The name slipped out involuntarily, but she only registered the fact hours later, when thinking back. 'And that's what he was saying to you just now?'

'Yes, I had to physically restrain him at one stage, and then he wept….'

'Then he knows now that there's no hope for Robbie?' The room was very quiet, and Sherie's throat was tight as a vice.

'Sometimes he accepts it, and sometimes he doesn't.' The paediatric oncologist shifted in his chair, as if trying to shake off the effect of his hour with the distraught father. 'Sometimes he just refuses to look at the situation at all…I think that makes it harder. I told him we had decided to discontinue treatment—other than palliative care, of course—and send Robbie home, and he accused me—us—of trying to cut down on our workload so we could get a Christmas break. Then I tried to talk to him about the hospice movement, which Princess Diana has been working hard to publicise, I've noticed, and he reacted as if I was proposing sending Robbie to some kind of medieval lunatic asylum.'

'He's been that way from the beginning, apparently,' Sherie nodded. 'We've been trying to help him express what he's feeling and start to work through it in some way, but he just seems to bottle everything up for a long time and then explode. It's as if he's trying to fight Robbie's battle for him…and we haven't been able to convince him to see a counsellor.'

'I gathered that,' nodded Richard.

'It makes *us* feel angry at times, against him, which is wrong.'

'But human.'

'Which is all we are, as I keep explaining without success to one or two of my nurses,' Sherie said drily.

A short shared laugh broke some of the tension they each felt.

'I don't think he will take legal action, or any of the other things he was threatening,' said Richard Brent. 'But I did think you ought to be warned.'

'Yes—I'm glad. Thank you for making the time,' Sherie said. 'We'll be aware of what's happened if he comes in. He's a likeable man, when he's not too bowed down by all this. And Robbie is a—well, an angel.'

'Is it wise to use that word?' he asked lightly.

Sherie reddened. 'No, it's not wise,' she said in a low tone. She thought again of their shared past. This was the man who had seduced her in New Zealand, left her pregnant and thus unknowingly forced her to face a battle with her parental instincts that was in it's way as difficult as that which Ken Williams was now going through.

What was the date today? The eighth. Seven years and two months to the day since she had signed the papers which had surrendered Simon up for adoption. And that had been only the beginning...

'Are our feelings ever wise?' she added ironically, after a tiny pause. She wanted to go on, but regained control and shut her well-drawn lips firmly to keep back the words.

'That's a dramatic statement,' Richard Brent remarked, rising to his feet in one economical movement. 'Is it based on your own wide experience of life?'

'Yes,' she said shortly, hating the sarcasm she heard in his tone.

'Whereas from my life, thus far, I've drawn more optimistic conclusions,' he said. 'I suppose we'll have to leave it at that.'

She struggled to find a reply to this, but before she did, he had moved to the door and stood looking back at her with his hand gripping the round metal knob. In his face she could read anger and frustration—and something else that she could not put a name to.

'I must go,' he said, his blue eyes cool and the smooth planes of his face immobile. 'But I'll be somewhere about for the rest of the day. Page me if you need to.'

'All right.' It came out ungraciously, though she had not intended it to, and before she could amend her expression in any way, he had gone, leaving her feeling stranded and dissatisfied, just as he had the other day in this same place.

In a reflex gesture, Sherie put a hand to her black hair and found that it had loosened into a halo of softness which was too untidy for a Ward Sister.

Slowly, she repaired the damage, glad of the chance to do something with her hands.

She had given him the wrong impression of her character. There was only this one streak of bitterness in her nature. She knew it, and knew also, even in the middle of a black mood, that there was a cure for it somewhere.

Did she regret anything that had happened? Any of that 'wide experience' Richard Brent had just spoken of so sarcastically? It did not take long to answer this question to her own satisfaction, as she had thought about it before. No, she did not have regrets. She had been formed by her past, its pain and its joy, it was a part of her now, and that meant there was a value to it.

Suddenly she knew what she had to do. She couldn't go on like this day after day, jeopardising a job she loved because of these unresolved feelings about her past. She couldn't wait until she made a slip of the tongue that would force things into the open, or till she goaded him by her prickly manner so that he was forced to speak himself. Tonight at home she would write him a note asking if they could arrange a private meeting. Or perhaps another opportunity would present itself in the course of the day. She knew, though, that it must not happen at the hospital. It must be on neutral ground, or perhaps on her own territory...

It wouldn't be easy. 'But I'm not going to be a coward about it. I'm not going to hide behind impotent anger forever, like Ken Williams is.'

So it was with a firm step and a new lightness of heart that she left the ward conference room. There was a fresh arrangement of bright flowers on the desk top at the nurses' station—maidenhair fern, baby's breath, and orange and yellow-toned roses. She took a moment to inhale their perfume deeply, then turned as a voice addressed her.

'Sherie! I was just coming to look for you,' Lisa Perry came towards her from the far corridor, her face clearing at the sight of her senior. 'West Six was asking if we could admit a Hodgkins' Disease this afternoon. They've got him down for a laparotomy tomorrow, and they thought they had room for him, but they haven't…on the ward, I mean. Someone else didn't get discharged. But he'd be coming over to us later anyway for radio and chemo, so I provisionally said…'

'Er…hang on,' Sherie went to the computer.

'Sorry,' Lisa said sheepishly, 'that didn't come out as clearly as I thought it was going to!'

'No, don't worry,' Sherie drawled in mock impatience. 'I extracted the main points successfully, I think.'

Carefully, she keyed in various coded phrases to obtain the information she needed about current and future occupancy in the ward. Obviously, it wasn't hard to count up the number of patients they had at the moment, but she had to know who would be coming in as well. Some could not be predicted in advance, of course—patients sent from country or Pacific Island hospitals which could not provide the expert and specialised treatment this hospital was famous for, and new metropolitan cases referred by GPs for tests. But others were known of some time beforehand—transfers from West Six, which handled the surgical side of Paediatric Oncology, and those children who came in at regular intervals for follow-up radiotherapy or drug treatment.

'Yes, we're fine,' she said, 'Three admissions that we know about this week, but Cindy and Paul will be gone in a day or two, and Helen Harris is going back to West Six.'

'Another op? Oh no!' Lisa grimaced her concern.

'Yes, Mr Marzouk decided this morning when he'd looked at her scan,' Sherie told her. 'But the outlook is still good, apparently. He's so confident that this one'll go really well, and there'll be no more to worry about.'

'That's great!' Lisa brightened at once. 'Do the parents know?'

'Yes, Mrs Harris was there when Mr Marzouk told me. She'll be in for the whole thing, and that really helps Helen.'

Although neither of them mentioned it, eleven-year-old Helen was not the most endearing child in the world, and had quite severe behaviour problems when her sensible and loving mother was not present. There was a good chance, though, that once she was back at home again, most of these problems would sort themselves out.

'Anything else?' asked Sherie.

'No, all's fine as far as I am concerned.' said Lisa. 'I'll ring East Six and confirm that we can take him. The parents are waiting to hear, and are anxious, of course.

She turned to the phone, and Sherie left the nurses' station to take a brief tour of the six rooms that contained the fifteen beds in the ward. Soon she would be making a much slower tour for the medication round, but that involved a very particular kind of concentration, and this time she wanted to check on the children themselves, not on the precise number of milligrams in their dosages.

Alison's laugh came from the activities room as Sherie passed it. The sound was a welcome one, suggesting that the girl was allowing her naturally sunny and lively temperament to blossom in front of her young patients.

Sherie felt a surge of satisfaction. Somehow she was determined to win through with Alison, and to help the girl herself win through—to become the well-rounded nurse she had the capacity to be, with many exciting career opportunities ahead of her.

What about Alison's personal life, though? Sherie could see that there was a battle to be fought there too. Did an outsider have any right to interfere? No…After all, she didn't really know the whole story. It seemed pretty clear that the infatuation was all on one side.

What would Richard say when Sherie confronted him? No, far better not to even think about it.

Ken Williams did not turn up at lunchtime as he had said he would. Sherie looked up from her desk in the nurses' station every time new footsteps sounded just out of sight along the corridor. She was skipping her meal break specially so that she could see him, commissioning Alison to bring back a packet of sandwiches and a piece of fruit, which incidentally ensured that the first-year herself would have a meal and a chance to sit down.

Finally at three the grief-stricken father appeared, and Sherie knew as soon as she saw him that he had at last begun to reach an inner peace and acceptance. Mrs Williams was with him, and though a heaviness beneath her eyes and lines etched around her mouth betrayed what she was going through, she seemed calm too.

Sherie rose and went to meet them, shepherding them straight into the small counselling room back along the corridor. It was Mrs Williams who spoke first.

'Dr Brent told Ken this morning that you wanted to send Robbie home.' Her voice broke a little on the last word, and her husband continued.

'It's what we want now too. I didn't at first, but we talked—I haven't been to work today—and we know now it's the best thing. He'll have his two big brothers…'

'And Christmas,' Mrs Williams put in. 'We're already thinking about how to make it extra special.'

Sherie nodded silently.

'But we need to know what we have to do for him,' Ken Williams said. 'I was bloody rude to Dr Brent today—I wouldn't listen to anything he had to say.'

'I can call him up very easily,' said Sherie.

'Yes, I'd like to apologise.' His square-cut features worked a little as he spoke and his sandy hair was raked aside with a rough, work-reddened hand. It was clear that he found any kind of emotional display very difficult. His entire body—stocky, solid—was set in angular shapes as if he met everything bull-headed and ready for a confrontation. To such a man, his impotence in the face of death would be an unusually hard thing to come to terms with.

'I didn't mean that you needed to apologise, I'm sure Richard understands…' Damn! Again she had used his name as if it was familiar to her. '…But there will be things he needs to talk over with you, to do with Robbie's care and treatment, as you said, and with what you can expect as time goes by.'

She reached for the phone and got on to the paediatric oncologist quite quickly.

'OK…good, see you in a few minutes, then.' Sherie replaced the receiver after her brief conversation with him, her words echoing back in her head. Hadn't she sounded unnaturally high-pitched during all that?

In Richard Brent's tone there had been relief and enthusiasm when she told him that Mr and Mrs Williams were here and wanted to discuss Robbie's treatment at home.

'He really cares,' she thought wonderingly. 'Somewhere at the back of his mind, this has been nagging at him all day, just as it's been nagging at me. If Mr and Mrs Williams hadn't come in, or if they'd still been angry and hostile, he would have gone home with it as I would, and spent all evening trying to shake it off, or think of a solution.'

While she made tea for the strain-wearied couple, she had time to analyze this change she saw in Richard Brent. Remarks that the young Richard had made eight year ago came back to her.

At the time she had managed to shut her eyes to them, then later Robyn had encouraged her to add them to her reasons for bitterness. Now she was simply surprised that the man seemed to have changed so much. Back then, he had talked of specialising only as a way of moving ahead, making a name for himself—not to mention the money—but now, Sherie could see and sense that he was working in paediatric oncology because he had something to offer, and a belief in what he could achieve.

Had he become more compassionate and caring in his personal life as well? But no! Hadn't she just vowed to block off this introspection?

She was crossing the corridor with the tea things when Richard arrived, breathing a little more heavily than normal as if he had hurried to get here. He must have come through the heat of the day from Outpatients across the road, as there was a mist of sweat on his forehead and temples that darkened some curls of hair at his hairline.

He looked far more relaxed than he had that morning. He halted only a pace from her and grinned down at her from his superior height, his eyes flicking quickly over her compact curved figure.

'Room on the tray for another cup?' The usual low drawl. He reached out and brushed a steady forefinger lightly along the finely-sculpted line of her jaw, and she froze.

'Yes, there is. Just a minute.' Her tone was brittle and cool. 'I'll take this in and then bring you one.'

'Fine,' He drew back into himself at once, retreating with an almost imperceptible shrug and a fluid turn on his heel into the room where Mr and Mrs Williams waited, talking in low voices together.

Sherie fumed as she went to get his cup. That touch, tiny though it had been, had invaded her sense of personal space in a way which she had not invited at all. And worse, her jaw still tingled where his smooth fingertip had made contact. The small voice of reason told her that if it had been anyone else, or someone she liked, at least, she wouldn't have minded, but because it was him, she did.

'Stay with us, Sister Page,' he said when she brought his tea. 'You're involved here.'

'It might be better if I call Judy Colton,' Sherie said quickly, glancing down at her fob watch, and referring to the incoming Ward Sister. 'She should have arrived by now, and she's been involved in caring for Robbie longer than I have, hasn't she?'

She appealed to Mr and Mrs Williams for confirmation, and they nodded, giving support unknowingly to her strategy for escaping from Richard Brent's presence. She left the room at once, and found that Judy had indeed arrived a few minutes ago, ready for the change of shift. The curly-haired

blonde nodded quietly when Sherie told her what was
going on.

'Well, we've known for a while that Robbie was
failing,' she said quietly. 'I'm glad Dr Brent thinks
home is the best place for him. Dr Murray was against
it in most cases, and sometimes I used to feel he was
wrong—humble nurse though I am.'

The dry line was typically Judy, and Sherie smiled.
She too had found Richard Brent's predecessor a little
too conservative in his views at times, although their
periods on this ward had overlapped by only a few
weeks.

Judy went to the counselling room and Sherie
gathered everyone together to give their reports to the
incoming staff, with a shy twenty-two-year-old nurse,
Debbie Gatkins, deputising for Sister Colton. The
change-over was smooth and unfussed, and when
Sherie was ready to go off, there were voices still
sounding faintly behind the closed door of the
counselling room as she passed it.

In the large and busy ground-floor concourse of the
hospital, a display outside one of the three
convenience boutiques caught her eye, and she
remembered several items she and Robyn needed at
home. It would be a little cheaper to stop at a
supermarket on the way, but the thought of spending
more time in her hot car, not to mention negotiating
parking lots and check-out queues, tempted her into
stopping here.

She regretted it ten minutes later as she made her
way to the staff car park.

She was sheltering from the heat beneath the
enormous Moreton Bay fig-trees which lined the
driveway that formed her route. Their umbrella-like
canopies were a thick frenzy of shiny deep green

leaves, providing total shade, but even so, it was still hot, and passing cars churned up eddies of dust in the dry beds of shrubbery nearby.

One passing car pulled to a smooth halt beside Sherie, and its driver called to her through the window, 'Need a lift?'

It was Richard Brent, behind the wheel of a late-model smoky-blue Toyota. A modest enough machine, but had he picked its colour to match his eyes? Sherie wondered with cynical inner humour.

'No, I don't, thanks,' she said to him, politely, but with an instinctive distance that she did not at first stop to question. 'I have my own car.'

'We could have a drink somewhere and I could drop you back later.'

'I don't think that's a good idea…she began.

It was awkward. The driveway was narrow, but he was on the opposite side, leaning a bare, tanned elbow along the lower edge of the open window. There were other people passing—visitors, staff coming off duty, or walking from building to building on various errands. Sherie felt exposed, although it was unlikely that anyone cared.

'What, washing your hair?' Richard drawled lightly, with one eyebrow raised.

'I didn't say I *couldn't*,' she retorted across the space that separated them, keeping her voice as low as she could and stepping out on to the bitumen, 'I said I thought it wasn't a good idea, and…'

She was about to add another heated retort when, ashamed, she remembered how firm her resolution had been this morning about confronting him. For several seconds she struggled against the voice inside her that said, 'Another time, not now. You've been working all day and you're tired. It doesn't matter if this drags on a bit longer, Another time.'

She saw that he was frowning at her, growing impatient, clearly regretting his spontaneous invitation, and about to drive on. It would be easy to let him do so, and never mind that he thought her gauche and rude, but suddenly she found her courage. He was already winding up his window with a rapid impatient movement, having reached to the centre of his dashboard to switch on the air-conditioning.

'Wait!' she blurted.

His hand paused in its action and then reversed direction. He switched off the air-conditioning too, and looked at her, waiting, his face neutral.

'I'd like to talk,' she said, willing her voice to remain steady, 'But not here, and not at a café or bar, I don't think. Would you come to my place?'

'To your place?' His blue eyes flashed in quickly-concealed surprise, and Sherie bit her lip. It must seem like an odd suggestion.

'Yes…just for a drink,' she nodded. 'If that's not too inconvenient…?'

'Well, if you think back a few minutes,' he drawled, 'it was actually me who asked you for a drink in the first place. Where do you live?'

'Kirribilli.'

'Nice,' He raised his eyebrows. 'And I'm in Mosman—no problem at all. Your place would be almost on my route.'

He noted down the exact address, using a page at the back of the neat note book he kept in his glove-compartment for recording mileage and petrol purchases.

'Straight away?' he added, when he had finished.

'I beg your pardon?'

'Well…would you like some time to

change…relax? I can easily do a few errands on the way to give you a head-start.'

'Yes, that would be good,' Sherie nodded.

'See you in a hour or so, then.' Again he wound up the window and had pulled away before she had time to do more than nod and smile briefly. Those last words had been very affably spoken, but that gave no accurate guide as to what he was really thinking.

CHAPTER FIVE

ROBYN was not at home when Sherie arrived, although they had been due to come off work at the same time. This often happened now that Robyn's involvement with Bernard was becoming serious. It was a relief, though; Sherie wanted to talk to Richard alone.

First she checked the fridge. Yes, there were cool drinks, milk for coffee or tea, cheese to go with cracker biscuits and some grapes to arrange on a glass fruit platter.

Next she took a refreshing cold shower, then hesitated over what to wear. It was still unseasonably hot, and the slight insipid breeze barely moved the leaves of the potted plants on the balcony.

Sherie's summer wardrobe badly needed revitalising, and as yet she hadn't managed to do it. She now wished fervently that it had been higher on the list of her priorities for her four days off. Two cool pretty dresses that she had worn over the weekend were now in her cane clothes basket waiting to be washed, as were a couple of summery blouses that might have teamed with skirts or silky trousers.

Wrapped in a fluffy towel, she stood in front of gaping cupboard doors and shifted coat-hangers to and fro aimlessly. There was a red dress, but it would look too formal, as if she'd gone to a great deal of trouble to dress up for him, and would require make-up, jewellery and heeled shoes. Or a casual summer suit in beige cotton...no, that wasn't right. The hem was coming down at the end of last summer, and she hadn't sewn it up again.

The batik-pattern of an Indonesian-style sarong in a sky blue, midnight blue and black caught her attention, and on impulse she pulled the folded tube of fabric off the hanger. It was temptingly cool...Too casual? Probably, but perhaps that was how she needed to be in order to get through the ordeal of confronting him with the consequences of their shared past.

Quickly she slipped out of the towel and knotted the simple wide tube above her breasts. It left her shoulders bare, and finished comfortably just below her knees. Worn with white sandals, a necklace of delicate white beads, and with her long hair tied in a high ponytail fastened with a crisp white bow clip, the outfit was completed.

Sherie felt satisfied with the results as she stood in the kitchen preparing cheese and pâté and crackers, as well as the grapes, and also a plate of macaroon biscuits that she had made on Friday. Lastly, she found a tin of smoked oysters and prepared a plate of those too. Food was an easy thing to hide behind, sometimes.

But while washing her hands in the bathroom she caught sight of her reflection in the mirror above the basin, and felt a wave of doubt sweep over her. Was 'casual' the wrong word altogether? Would Richard think she was trying to be provocative?

In sudden panic she began to undo the knotted fabric, tearing a fingernail at the corner as she did so. It would have to be the cotton suit. She would pin up the hem...

The doorbell rang just as she succeeded in untying the knot, and she clutched at the fabric as it slipped down her torso, pressing it in a crumpled handful against her chest. It was him! It had to be, and changing was now out of the question.

A bright golden and green shaft of late afternoon light met her at the door, and blocking part of it, the tall figure of Richard Brent. He, of course, still wore this morning's pale grey trousers and open-necked shirt, its sleeves rolled to the elbows to display sinewy tanned forearms. It was a casual enough outfit, but not when compared to her own simple wrap of cotton.

'Hullo. Come in.'

She stood aside, and he stepped in, then she shut the door and he followed her, his strides firm and confident. Trying to be surreptitious, Sherie pulled at the front of her sarong, which had already worked down a little, revealing the first creamy hint of the hollow between her breasts. That second knot she had hurriedly tied was not nearly as firm as the first.

'Been to Bali?' The laconic oblique reference to her action made her blush, and she was thankful that he was still behind her.

'No, it was a present,' she replied rather thinly. 'Some friends went last year.'

'Suits you.'

'I only wear it in the house. Most of my clothes are in the wash, and it's so hot, I'm sorry.'

'There's really no need to apologise...it looks delightful,' he insisted, and Sherie stiffened. He *did* think she was setting the stage for a flirtation! Or a resumption of their old affair.

But could she blame him? First, inviting him here when he had suggested the neutral atmosphere of a café-bar, and now appearing at the door in this.

What an idiot she had been not to have spent the past half an hour putting up that hem, instead of fiddling about in the kitchen preparing elaborate hors d'oeuvres!

'What can I offer you to drink?' she asked thinly, taking refuge in the bland duties of a hostess. 'There's fruit juice, iced coffee, or something stronger—brandy and dry ginger…'

'Iced coffee sounds perfect,' he interrupted.

He stood in the doorway that led to the balcony while she prepared a tall glass for each of them, his straight nose visible only in tanned profile as he half turned towards the sweeping vista of the Harbour.

'You have a magnificent view,' he commented.

'Yes, we do. It's one of the main reasons my father bought this place.'

'Oh, it's your father's?'

'Yes.'

'He lives here too?'

'No, but we pay rent to him for it.'

'Who's we?'

'None of your business,' she could have retorted, but didn't. 'Myself and another nurse,' she said instead. 'Robyn.' There was no sense in alienating him now, when…

When what? When in a few minutes, or in half an hour, depending on how long it took her to drum up the courage to actually face him and say what she had to say, he would have plenty of reason to feel all sorts of things.

Just what *would* he feel? A flash of memory came to her…all those months and months when she had still hoped that he would turn up, and the dreams she had allowed herself…One day the phone would ring, it would be Richard and an hour later she would be in his arms. 'We'll get married,' he would say. 'Oh, my darling…'

How long had she gone on having those dreams? Far *too* long. And as if his response would be anything like that, after all this time! As if she would *want* it to be!

She finished preparing the iced coffee, and brought the plate of hors d'oeuvres out to the small square wooden coffee table that stood in the centre of the room on the fading pile of a once-magnificent Persian rug, gleaned from a family attic.

Richard sat down and leaned forward to take coffee and a cracker, and suddenly, very forcefully, Sherie was aware of his flagrant maleness. Dark hair showed at the opening of his shirt, and his arms were held in a way that emphasised the powerful muscles of his shoulders. Trying to be discreet, she tightened the knot that held up her sarong, and wished at the very least that she was wearing more beneath it than a brief pair of pink cotton underpants.

She took her own coffee and a macaroon, then sat opposite him, in the grey fabric-armchair that matched the couch he had chosen. This was the moment, it would be ridiculous and awkward to put it off any longer. He was already gazing at her, a speculative question in his heavy-lashed blue eyes.

'I think you know why I asked you to come,' she said.

'No, I don't,' he answered, after a gulp of cream-topped coffee. 'Was there a reason? A specific one, I mean?'

'Obviously there was,' Sherie retorted. It was clear that he hadn't decided to make this easy for her. 'I'd scarcely ask a senior doctor to my own flat after less than a week together on the ward without a reason. Please stop this pretence!'

'What pretence, Sister Page?' He was wary now,

which was perhaps not surprising. Her tone had begun to betray the underlying hostility she could not rid herself of.

'Richard…didn't my name or my face ring any bells when Alison introduced us?' asked Sherie. 'Haven't they rung any bells since?'

'We've met before, I take it,' he said cautiously, as if he thought that perhaps he was dealing with a woman who was slightly out of control. The tension now in the air seemed so incongruous in the bright, sunny flat that for a second Sherie almost laughed, then emotion took hold of her and she burst out.

'We've more than met, Richard. You fathered my child…eight years ago in New Zealand. You never knew that, though. How could you? You never contacted me again once we got back to Sydney and you hadn't given me your address or phone number, so I had no way of contacting you…'

She was on her feet now, her coffee back on the table scarcely touched, and her fingers clasped together to keep them from shaking. Richard was leaning back, pressing himself hard against the back of the couch as if bracing himself against her attack. Apart from the one shocked sound that had escaped his lips, he had not spoken.

'I spent nine months of pregnancy waiting for you, expecting you, then making excuses for you,' Sherie went on in a low, trembling voice. 'Oh, the theories I manufactured as to why you hadn't turned up! I used to tell Robyn, "He's had an accident…There's been a death in the family…He's lost my address." I even advertised twice in case that had happened, tried to get hold of the student list from Newcastle Medical School, but of course they wouldn't give it to me. I had so much faith that you'd really cared. It wasn't until

Simon was actually born that I faced the fact that you didn't want to see me again. Robyn had been sceptical all along, and finally I saw she was right. She's been invaluable—the perfect friend—from the beginning. I decided to adopt Simon out…for his sake it seemed the only thing to do. I didn't want to risk venting any bitterness on him…'

'Sherie, Sherie, we must stop this!' Richard was on his feet now too, and had crossed the space that separated them in a couple of long strides. He tried to take her by the shoulders and pull her into his arms, but she resisted fiercely, twisting away from him and folding her arms across her chest.

'Yes, all right,' he said immediately. 'That was stupid. Of course you don't want to be touched. But listen, there's a mistake. Whoever the father of your child is…

'Was' Sherie blurted harshly.

'Was?'

'Simon died…in a foster home. The adoption had been going ahead as planned. The adoptive parents were waiting for him, and I changed my mind…I couldn't go through with it. I knew I'd been wrong to think I'd feel bitter towards Simon. I loved him with all my heart. I'd already postponed starting my nursing training for a year, but I decided that even if it meant waiting several more years till he was at school, and struggling with supporting mother's benefit and odd unskilled jobs…or telling my father all about it and getting support from him, I was going to keep him. The children's welfare people…understandably…wanted to be sure that I really meant it, the whole thing was still hanging in the balance, and he was in a temporary foster…home when…he died. A cot death. Or Sudden Infant Death Syndrome, as I should call it, as I'm a nurse. It kills one baby in five hundred in Australia, and they still don't know why…'

'But, Sherie,' Richard said gently, 'you've made a mistake. It wasn't me. Whatever reason you have for thinking it was, you're wrong, and we'd better get it all cleared up straight away. This thing has been burning away inside you, and we need to solve it, but to do that we have to get things straight. You said this happened in New Zealand eight years ago, but I've never been to New Zealand in my life.'

Trembling, Sherie came to herself and looked at him. His forehead was deeply creased and his dark brows had lowered over his blue eyes. Did she believe him? He was studying her with the same intensity, and for a long moment there was silence between them. Richard was the first to speak.

'I was in Africa eight years ago, working as a doctor for the Australian Volunteers Abroad programme,'

'How old are you?' she asked him.

'Thirty-four.'

'And where did you train?'

'Melbourne.'

Suddenly the strength began to drain from Sherie's legs and she had to put a hand to the back of the couch to steady herself. He saw the action and came to her, holding out his arms. Without questioning anything, she went into the cradling circle of warmth he had created and he held her.

Her face pressed into his firm shoulder and his hands massaged and caressed her back. She didn't want to think, or to feel anything but his warmth and firmness, his cheek against her hair, and the steady rhythm of breathing in his chest. But after several minutes he drew back and led her to the couch, putting the brimming glass of coffee in her hand. It spilled a little, and a cold runnel of milky brown liquid ran down her hand and wrist.

'Drink!' he commanded gently. 'I suppose it should be hot tea rather then cold coffee, but it can't be helped.'

He laughed a little, and coaxed a smile from her. Obediently, she took a gulp of the coffee, then transferred it to her other hand and licked up the trickle of liquid on her wrist.

'His name was Richard Brent too, I take it,' Richard said. He had sat down beside her and was still studying her carefully.

'Yes, and he'd just finished his medical finals.'

'A Newcastle student?'

'Yes.'

'He must be younger than me.'

'He'd be thirty-two now.'

'But there must be a considerable similarity in our looks.'

'In your height and colouring. I was surprised at how much you seemed to have changed, but I put that down to shorter hair, no moustache, no glasses. Of course I should have realised but...'

'But that name meant so much to you, it blinded you.'

'Something like that,' she admitted.

'So you believe me?'

Sherie laughed shakily. 'Yes, I do.'

'And how does it feel?'

'Don't ask me yet!'

'Is it time for me to leave?' asked Richard. 'After all, I'm here under false pretences now...Or would you like to have dinner? Actually I have two subscription tickets to the theatre tonight. We're early, we could fit in both.'

'It sounds lovely.' Sherie told him.

'I think you need it…Sherie, is this the first time you've really   talked about this? To an outsider I mean?' Richard asked quietly.

'Yes, I suppose it is,' she answered slowly. 'I've never even told my father. He was away in Saudi Arabia…he works for an oil company…for a year and half. My class at school wasn't a close group. Robyn is the only one I kept in touch with, and of course she knows everything. My other friends are all from nursing, and by the time I started my course, it was all over.'

'But Robyn has been a sterling support?'

'Oh, yes,' Sherie said at once. But the 'yes' had fallen a little as if she was in doubt, and he picked up on it.

'Perhaps too much of a support?' he probed gently.

'Just lately…I haven't known what to feel,' she answered slowly. 'But you're right. That's it. It's as if she doesn't want me to forget, or put it behind me. She's still…almost too indignant on my behalf.'

Sherie laughed and stood up, suddenly wary about how much she was telling this man. 'But she's my best friend. Perhaps it *isn't* her at all….Perhaps it's just me. And if we're going to have dinner, I'd better change. I can't go like this.'

'What about me?' Richard spread his hands apologetically and grinned, 'I have my suit jacket in the car. Will that do?'

'Do you think I'm expecting tails and a silk cummerbund?' Sherie returned lightly.

She left him and went to her room, the sarong making a dull cotton swish sound as she walked in it. Her bare shoulders didn't seem to matter now. The room was bright with late afternoon sun, and a distorted rectangle of light struck on the wall above her bed.

Sherie went to the venetian blind, pulled it down, and closed the slats, because the room was hot, but then she found that she didn't want to shut out the brightness completely. Talking to Richard had taken an enormous weight off her soul, and the light in the room was a symbol for the refreshing lightness in her heart.

She *had* been bottling all this up for too long. Meeting this Richard Brent and finding that, after all, he was not the man who had hurt her, had done something important. It had made her see that she couldn't go on waiting for fate to make a neat end to this whole thing. She would probably never encounter the Richard Brent from New Zealand, never have a chance to confront him with what had happened. And perhaps it was best that way. She could find her own peace and resolution. It was all in the past now.

Sherie opened the wardrobe door and saw the red dress that she had rejected earlier. It seemed appropriate now. It was the bridesmaid's outfit she had worn when a nursing friend, Barbara, who was now living in Perth, had got married last spring.

The heavy dark red shantung silk had complemented the sophisticated gown that Barbara had chosen, but on its own it didn't look like a bridesmaid's dress. Sherie pulled it out and heard its satisfying rustle. With dangling ruby earrings, matching necklace, bracelet and dark red shoes, filmy stockings, touches of soft warm colour to her eyes and mouth, hair pulled gently into a glossy ponytail and fastened with a frivolously glittering clip, a nuance of perfume…

The admiring flash in Richard's eyes twenty minutes later told Sherie that she had made a good choice. Behind him, she noticed that their half-drunk coffees and scarcely-touched plates of hors d'oeuvres had been cleared away. He saw her glance and answered the unworded question.

'I hope I've disposed of everything properly,' he said. 'Plastic wrap over the plates of biscuits. Fruit and pâté and cheese back in the fridge.'

'We didn't do very well with it all, did we?' she smiled.

'I'd venture to say that you made rather too much,' he answered.

'Distracting myself from nerves,' she explained. It was such a relief to be honest! None of the other men she had been out with over the past six years had known anything about the fact that she had borne and lost a child. And now to find out that Richard Brent knew and seemed to accept it!

A warning bell jangled in her head. She wasn't going out with Richard Brent! They were having dinner together, but that was all.

'I've been thinking about restaurants,' he said as they walked to the door. 'Any preferences?'

'Somewhere by the water,' she answered without thinking, then added, 'But anywhere you've thought of is fine.'

'By the water' could imply both expensive and intimate, and she didn't want him to think she was building anything into this occasion at all. She wondered how he came to have a spare ticket at such short notice.

'I thought it might be best to go to the Wharf, since that's where the play is. I used your phone while you were changing—I hope that's all right?'

'Of course.'

'And I managed to get a booking.'

He made no attempt to take her arm as they went down the shrub-lined path that ran through the jungly mass of garden to the street. Sherie was glad. She led the way and arrived well ahead. Richard stopped to examine a riotously flowering hibiscus.

They reached the car, and as she slid into the softly-upholstered passenger seat, less relaxed, suddenly, now that she was alone in the car with him, Sherie searched feverishly in her mind for a safe subject. Nothing presented itself immediately, and her companion seemed to be having the same trouble.

Richard had reached into the back seat and taken the neatly laid out grey suit jacket before taking his place behind the wheel, rolling down his shirt sleeves and buttoning them at the cuffs, then shrugging his strong shoulders into the garment.

'Nice evening,' was all he said as they pulled out into the street.

'Yes, there's going to be a lovely sunset later on, I think.'

Silence again. It was a very comfortable car, at least, and Sherie was lulled and relaxed by his smooth, capable driving. As they wound through Kirribilli and up towards the Harbour Bridge, she turned from the view of the city and caught sight of his hands strong and tanned, with finely-sculpted sinews. They were the hands of a mature man, she realised, and she wondered for a moment about his relationship with Alison Grace. The girl was only just over half his age…

It was strange, she did not have the impression of him as someone who would enjoy 'cradle-snatching'. A more equal relationship seemed more his style.

He had worked in Africa, seen a lot, and no doubt had experience with women.

Surely he needed a woman who had tasted more of life's realities than Alison could have in her no doubt sheltered eighteen years?

'Penny for them,' said Richard, startling her.

'Oh...I was just wondering if you knew anything more about the play,' she improvised quickly. It was impossible to answer truthfully about what she had been thinking.

'No, I don't' he replied calmly. 'I have a subscription ticket, so I just turn up on the designated night. Sometimes we don't even know what we're going to see. I think that's the case with a lot of subscribers. This is a new Australian play, that's all I know.'

'Right.'

She had noticed his use of 'we'. Did that mean he had a regular companion at the theatre? Where was she tonight? Was it Alison? Somehow, Sherie thought not. Did Richard Brent have more than one woman in his life at the moment, then? Not her concern, of course.

They parked easily at this hour, then walked down the long walkway in rhythmic unison. He moved well for such a powerful man, Sherie noticed, very aware of him at her side.

The Wharf restaurant was still bright with the sunlight that danced and dazzled on the water which surrounded it on three sides, yet the salt-tanged air was cool and refreshing, kept circulating as it was by large ceiling fans.

They each chose a tasty cold entreé followed by pasta with a light sauce, and imaginatively-created salad. A bottle of Chablis added zest and richness to the meal, and Sherie could not help being aware that female glances strayed to their table quite frequently. They had been placed near the floor-to-ceiling windows overlooking the water and Luna Park beyond, and it felt almost like being on board ship.

It was a restaurant full of well-dressed, attractive, and even well-known people, yet Sherie and her companion more than held their own as a couple.

'She thinks I'm lucky to be with him. She's envying me because she thinks we're in love,' Sherie realised as she caught the gaze of one young woman who sat with three much older people at a nearby table, her expression cross-hatched with ill-concealed boredom and discontent.

Then she realised that Richard was looking at her, a questioning smile of curiosity playing gently around the smooth bow of his lips.

'I'm admiring the fashions,' she said, to excuse her wandering gaze. She was behaving as badly as the girl at the next table, but after all the talking she had done at Kirribilli she now couldn't seem to think of anything to say.

Fortunately, Richard did not seem uneasy about it.

'You don't need to envy anyone here,' he replied to her explanation, surprisingly serious in tone. 'There's nothing you should want to change about how you look.'

'Thank you!'

As if he regretted the intensity of the compliment, or had noticed her discomfort at their silence, he suddenly launched into questions. What made her take up nursing? Did she like this hospital? Was it where she had trained? Had she any intention of going into nursing education later on? Had she always lived in Sydney?

At first the whole thing was very one-sided—he asked and she answered, but gradually this changed, and she was drawing him out too, then listening,

fascinated, to his account of the two years he had spent
in Africa with the Australian Volunteers Abroad
programme.

'And I've recently returned from another two-year
stint there,' he told her as they finished their wine.
'This time as a cancer specialist, helping them to set
up a modern unit in Harare. People only think of
medicine in Africa in terms of tropical diseases,
treating the effects of famine, and that sort of thing,
but areas we think of as very "Western", like cancer
and heart disease, need to be considered too. And
anything that encourages African doctors who have
trained overseas to return and work there in their own
countries is a step forward, in my opinion.'

Sherie nodded, 'And is that happening? Do the
doctors come back?'

'Some do, some don't' he answered. 'It's getting
better than it used to be.'

They had not even begun to think about dessert and
coffee when the bells rang to signal that the play would
shortly begin.

'I've forgotten all about how this evening started,'
Sherie realised as they stood amongst the press of
people waiting for their tickets to be checked. Richard
was close beside her, and she was suddenly aware of
the touch of his hand on her bare forearm. He himself
was not conscious of it, it was simply that his arm was
at rest at his side, but the slight touch was warm and
intimate somehow, and his capable shoulder above her
own seemed like a supporting buttress that she would
like to lean against.

She saw a woman ahead of her doing so, just laying
her head on her husband's shoulder for a moment,
needing no explanation or preamble or apology. It
would be so nice to have that kind of thing in her life.

This awareness in Sherie did not dissipate as the play progressed. Although she found the scenes and the story intriguing, absorbing and amusing, she was never oblivious of the man at her side. Indeed, she was conscious of every move he made, and when his arm shared the arm-rest between them with her own, she was shocked at the response of her senses.

At the end of the play, when applause broke out loudly, the release from her feelings that this gave Sherie was vastly satisfying, and she was one of the last to stop clapping.

'You liked it?' asked Richard. 'My mother finds some of the things here a bit modern for her taste.'

'Very much.' Not quite true. It was not that she *hadn't* liked it, but rather that for minutes at a time she was far more aware of the man at her side than the actors on stage. And it was his mother who usually had the other ticket!

'Disturbing, though, in parts, and thought-provoking,' she added.

'Yes.' This was a description that could apply to her own feelings at the moment as well.

'Would you like supper?' he asked.

'Yes, that would be lovely.'

She hoped he was sincere in the invitation, and not just asking out of politeness. She had accepted without thinking that perhaps he'd done enough for her this evening.

But Richard smiled frankly at her as he stood aside for her to pass out of the row of seats, then a warm hand came to her elbow and around her shoulders. She was flooded with longing and need, and with a strange sense of belonging. Was it just because she had unburdened herself to him this afternoon?

It was dangerous, whatever its source was, part of

her said—that part of her which still had its defences
well in place. When they came to a point where the
departing crowd was pressed close together, Sherie
took the opportunity to slide out of the warmth and
weight of his arm, and on their way down the steps he
did not try to hold her to him again.

They sat at the same table as before, only now it was
dark, and the black surface of the water shimmered
with light reflected from the ferris wheels and
roller-coasters of Luna Park and the neon signs of
North Sydney. Then a huge ship chuddered past,
bound for who knew where, its vast metal sides
seemingly only yards away from where they sat, and
its decks and cabins lit.

'Look, you can actually read its name from here,'
Richard pointed out. 'Or you could, if it was in
English.'

'Yes, is that the Cyrillic alphabet?' Sherie hazarded.

'I think it might be,' he nodded.

They watched in silence as it passed beneath the
massive arch and platform of the Harbour Bridge, then
Richard spoke again.

'It's a magnificent harbour we've got for ourselves,
isn't it?'

'I love it.' Sherie admitted.

'It's got everything—cityscapes, wild headland
parks, ships and fishing trawlers and yachts, houses
and gardens running down to the waterfront...'

'The zoo...'

'And this restaurant is hard to beat.'

'We should form a Sydney Harbour fan club,'
Sherie suggested lightly.

'We should!'

They both laughed, and then the waiter came with
the bill. It broke the shared moment of pleasure and

Sherie realised it was late. There were only a few groups still lazing at tables or loitering by the bar. She had an afternoon shift tomorrow, but still…

Richard seemed to have come to the same realisation, and in only a few minutes they were making their way along the roughly-planed wooden walkway that led back from the water to the street.

'I like the way they've kept the character of this place,' he said. 'The original wood, and traces of bitumen on the planks. No one could doubt that this was a working wharf for a long time.'

But the comment was a little absent, and Sherie only murmured her agreement. Their conversation was thin yet not strained as they drove back to Kirribilli. The traffic was light and the journey was fast. When Richard's car stopped outside her flat, it seemed to Sherie that the drive had been too short, and she did not want the evening to end.

He switched off the engine, and they sat there, the silence between them broken only by the ticking of cooling metal beneath the car bonnet.

'So…' he said lightly. 'Feeling OK about everything?'

'What do you mean?'

'I mean that you've told me quite a lot about yourself tonight…more than you've told anyone for a long time, it seems. Is it all right?'

'Very.'

Before she realised it was happening, he had taken her in his arms and cradled her against his chest. She could feel the vibration as he spoke in a low throaty tone. 'Any time you want to talk again…'

'No.'

'Don't let yourself go on bottling it up inside.'

Sherie stiffened. She could feel tears pricking

behind her eyes as she had a surge of all the old feelings—bruised and broken trust, grief for Simon, an inability to get close to any man. Richard's arms tightened around her and she found she was telling more to him about these things, but this time between broken and struggling sobs. When finally she quietened and was calm, there seemed little for either of them to say.

'I'll walk you to the door,' he told her.

'There's no need.'

But he was out of the car before she could protest further. The evening air suddenly struck a chill on her bare arms and open neck after the warmth of his car and of his arms. Dew must be falling, and the jungle-like foliage of the garden threw off dampness too.

Glancing up, Sherie saw a light go off in Robyn's room, so that their flat was in darkness apart from the small outside lamp which Robyn had left on for her. It was half hidden by a luxuriant monstera plant, so that the little porch that led to their front door was bathed only in a dim yellowish light.

Arriving there, with Richard still at her side, Sherie fumbled stupidly in her evening bag for the key. It seemed to take forever to poke around amongst the jumble of loose coins, a comb and a lipstick, and in the end it was futile. Just as she remembered she had left it in another bag, Richard's hand came down gently on her own to restrain her awkward fingers.

'It doesn't matter just yet,' he said.

She did not look up at him, aware that her fingers were still imprisoned caressingly in his own. Then his hand moved up to her face, moulding the line of her jaw softly and bringing her chin up. Before she realised quite what was happening, before she had time to even ask herself what she wanted, let alone what was wise, his lips had touched her skin, travelling tantalisingly from her cheek to her throat and then to her full mouth.

His arms slid around her and his hands explored the curves of her hips and thighs, finding the places where they met the warmth and hardness of his own lean limbs and torso.

With a longing that was almost like pain coursing through her, Sherie melted against him and surrendered to the overpowering need for this contact between them, after everything she had said to him tonight.

This kiss could have been the first one she had ever had, it was so fresh and sweet now, so unrelated to any rules or restrictions, or to that guard she had been unable to break down for so long, and which he had seemed to understand. His hand came up to her hair and loosened the high ponytail from its frivolous clip. His fingers threaded through the glossy dark mass and coaxed it down around her shoulders so that now, encircled by his body and protected by her own hair, she was completely warmed. The honey perfume of her shampoo mingled with the crisper male fragrance of his skin, and it seemed as if their kiss was a moment suspended out of time, an image captured frozen in a film. He was the one to break the wordless union between them, nuzzling her ear with the words:

'Is this what you needed?'

It wasn't the right thing to say. Sherie froze and pushed against his hard chest with her fingers.

'Sherie?'

'So this has been a counselling session, has it?' she demanded. 'You decided I needed a therapist, and you were prepared to fill the role!'

'No! Don't be silly, Sherie.'

'I'm not,' she said sharply. 'Let's stop now.'

Richard was silent for a moment. His eyes had narrowed and he was holding himself stiffly, his hands a little away from the sides of his body. Then he spoke. 'You'd like me to leave?'

'Yes, please, Thank you for a wonderful evening....I'm sorry.'

'Sorry for what? Don't apologise, Sherie.'

'Please go.' she muttered.

'I'll wait till you're safely in, at least.'

'I've forgotten my key. Robyn will let me in,' she said hollowly.

'Is she home?' he asked.

'I saw her light go off as we arrived, but she's probably still awake, I'll ring the bell.'

'You don't want me to wait?'

'No, don't trouble yourself.'

'It's no trouble,' he insisted.

'Don't, anyway.'

'Fine,' he nodded, apparently without regret. He seemed to have shrugged off her accusation about his motives. 'I'll see you quite soon, no doubt.'

On that note, he left. Sherie dared to watch him until he reached the bottom of the path, then he turned to look back up. Quickly, she flinched her gaze away and rang the doorbell, two short peals and then a longer one, which was a signal she and Robyn used if ever they needed to be let in late at night.

As she waited, facing determinedly away from the direction of the street, she heard the regular throb of Richard's car engine start up, swell, then fade away as he drove into the distance.

Inside the flat there was a clatter and a mild groan, the hall light came on, and Robyn's tired face appeared through a narrow opening in the door.

'Forgot my key—sorry,' said Sherie, and Robyn only nodded.

CHAPTER SIX

WHAT did the clock say? Three a.m.? And Sherie doubted that she had slept at all. For a long time she had just lain in twisted sheets staring at the immobile grey shadows on the ceiling, reliving Richard's kiss both with unwilling yearning and bitter regret. Why had she told him so much? It made her so vulnerable now.

When at last she had closed her eyes, all she had been able to see were memories playing before her inner vision like a film—the windy spring day when she had finally decided to try and get Simon back, her dry-eyed and outwardly calm meetings with counsellors, the tension-fraught rendezvous with the adoptive parents who were already waiting to take him into their lives—and then that devastating interference of fate, which had taken the decision out of all their hands.

And now Richard Brent knew all about it. There was nothing logical to this feeling of nakedness she now had, but that didn't make it any the less strong.

And she would have to see Richard again so soon.

Judy was on this morning, though, thank goodness...At last, it was this thought that relaxed her into sleep.

It was eleven before she woke, and on the roof was the sound of cool rain. A change must have come sweeping in suddenly across the Harbour during the night after summer's recent rehearsal. Cloud lay in scarves and billows in the sky, making a pattern of different greys, and the tropical foliage in the garden dripped and sighed.

Somehow this weather made the day easier, acting like
a protective wrap, as did the neat navy cardigan Sherie
wore over her blue uniform. Her night's sleep had not
been refreshing, but the damp, faintly sea-tanged breeze
was, and she felt thoroughly ready for work at
mid-afternoon when she arrived on the ward for the start
of her shift.

Things always looked black at three in the morning,
didn't they?

'There's an admission expected down from the country
this afternoon,' Judy Colton reported during the shift
change-over conference. 'She's eight years old,
leukaemia, radio and chemo, and her name's Storm
Sinclair.'

'Storm?' echoed Sherie.

'Yes, and she's got a big sister Shadow, and a little
brother Winter. The family lives on some kind of
commune up on the north coast.' Judy made a
disapproving face. 'Dr Brent's got the rest of the case
notes from the GP but it says here she's a vegetarian.'

'Well, there's nothing wrong with that,' said Sherie.

'No, I suppose not,' Judy admitted. 'But I must say the
combination of that and the names and where they
live…I'm surprised they're not trying to cure her with
herbs and crystals and aura massage!'

'What on earth is aura massage?' asked Melissa
Thomas, giggling.

'Oh, you know…' Judy answered vaguely. 'You zoom
your hands all around their bodies about four inches from
the skin, and that's supposed to intuitively tell you which
bits need healing. Then you do that by fiddling around
with bits of pink quartz.'

Although Sherie didn't share all Judy's prejudices
against New Age fads and treatments, she did allow

herself a faint smile at how easy the family of five were to identify. Jane Sinclair, in her late thirties, had long loose hair and a long loose skirt of hand-dyed cloth, while her tall, thin husband Terry, similar in age, sported a full bushy beard the colour of bleached tobacco, and khaki canvas work pants.

Storm was pale and thin, and as Judy had jokingly predicted, she *did* clutch in her hand a multi-faceted amethyst-coloured crystal that was really very beautiful.

Winter and Shadow, her brother and sister, were well-behaved, and seemed robust and healthy.

Terry Sinclair was clearly the spokesman for the family. While his wife was involved in keeping the three children entertained, and then in settling Storm into her four-bed room, he went through the details of Storm's personal and medical history with Sherie, watching closely as she filled in each item on several forms.

'We're not at all happy about this,' he said, pushing his bearded chin forward aggressively and leaning bony elbows on the desk. 'It's been proved that cancer has emotional causes, and can be cured through diet and meditation. Jane's accepted this hospital treatment for Storm now, but I warn you I haven't, and I'm going to make a nuisance of myself.'

Sherie looked up in surprise at the frank admission, and saw that there was a speculative glint in the man's blue eyes. He was studying her carefully, waiting for a response.

'That suits us,' she answered quickly. 'If by that you mean that you're going to be spending time with Storm at the hospital.'

'More than that,' said Terry Sinclair, 'Jane has to get back to the farm with Shadow and Winter, but I'll be here constantly. Her diet, for example…'

'Yes, it says here in the notes we received that your family is vegetarian,' Sherie put in. 'That's no problem. The dietician will be around later this afternoon and can plan a balanced diet with you.'

'What? A hospital's idea of a vegetarian diet?' he jeered with a laugh. 'Lettuce and tomato and processed cheddar cheese? No, thank you!'

'Hardly just that…' Sherie began, but Terry Sinclair continued derisively.

'We're vegans. Do you know what that means? No animal products at all, and only living plant food and protein-rich grains and pulses, I'll be preparing all Storm's meals myself and bringing them in for her, and I'll want to take her through four hours of meditation every day.'

He glared at Sherie, and, unwisely, she rose to the challenge.

'Please consider that Storm is just one patient on this ward, Mr Sinclair,' she said.

'So you're saying I can't do any of that?'

'No, I'm not,' Sherie began hastily. To be honest, she didn't know what she was saying. Who would be the person to make such a decision? As Ward Sister, was she to decide what level of disruption the ward could tolerate? Or did this come under more wide-reaching dictates of hospital policy? Could she pass the buck, in other words?

'Anything I can help with here?' It was Richard Brent. Sherie felt an icy thread tingle in her spine.

She hadn't heard him coming. Did he wear those soft rubber-soled shoes deliberately? She had been hoping against hope that she wouldn't encounter him today. His kiss last night, and the naked awareness she had of how much he knew about her now…

He was looking at her with a smile of empathy and reassurance that made her want to spit angry words at him. Last night hadn't created any kind of special relationship between them, and if he thought it had, then she would have to quickly make him think again.

'Everything's fine, thank you,' she said to him, 'Mr Sinclair and I are just going through Storm's details and discussing her diet.'

'Ah yes—Storm,' said Richard Brent, and pulled up a brown vinyl-covered chair. He was dressed casually but attractively as usual—white coat over white shirt with sleeves rolled to the elbows, and black pants with a paler fleck in the weave.

'You're Dr Brent,' Terry Sinclair said, glancing at the name badge pinned to the paediatric oncologist's lapel. 'You're going to be Storm's doctor down here.'

'Yes,' Richard nodded. 'Although not exclusively. She'll see other people from time to time as well.

'I want to get it straight about her diet—' Terry began.

He had turned away from Sherie now, as if giving up on her totally, and was focusing his steady blue gaze on Richard instead. Sherie looked down at the forms she had been filling out. Everything was done now.

'Sherie?' Melissa Thomas came over. 'Brendan McCarthy seems very distressed this afternoon....'

'Poor little Bren,' said Sherie standing. 'I'm not needed here.'

She was glad of the chance to get away. On her way down to Brendan's room at Melissa's side, she saw Jane Sinclair and the three children outside the door of the end room. They had unpacked Storm's things into cupboards beside her new bed, and seemed to be talking about ways to make the alien environment seem more like home.

'You'll bring my possum puppet next time you come

down, won't you, Mummy?' Sherie heard Storm say, beseeching and anxious.

'Of course, I will, darling,' Jane replied. 'We were silly to leave him home, weren't we?'

There was little Sherie could do for Brendan, she found. His general outlook was very good, he would be spending three weeks at home over Christmas, and his parents were very happy, but the chemotherapy that was slowly but surely ridding his body of abnormal white blood cells was also debilitating him severely at the moment, and at times it got too much for the small ten-year-old.

Sherie sat beside him, for as long as her busy schedule would allow, stroking the pale face and thin shoulders, and telling him any little anecdotes and stories that might distract him from nausea and dizziness. His mother and father spent as much time as they could with him, but today was their daughter's end-of-term concert, and it was important, as always, that other children in the family did not feel neglected because of a brother or sister's illness.

Brendan was a lonely prisoner in his unhappy little body today, but there would be a break soon at Christmas, and within a year the treatment should have stopped for good.

'Sherie…' It was Richard who interrupted her time with Brendan ten minutes later. He was standing in the doorway of the four-bed room where Brendan lay. 'I've got to go. Do you want to walk with me to the lift?'

Was this a professional request? Sherie wondered, as she left Brendan and went out of the room with the paediatric oncologist.

'I think I can wangle it about Storm Sinclair's diet and meditation,' he said to her in a confidential tone as they walked down the vinyl-corridor. 'It's pretty unorthodox, but…'

He laid a hand briefly on her shoulder, and Sherie flinched at the touch which she had welcomed so strongly last night.

'Don't say *that* to me!' she replied quickly. He really did think he'd established rights over her after last night…the rights of someone who knows another's secrets. Well, that was not the case! '*I'm* not in favour of the diet!'

'Aren't you?' It was a light question.

'No, I think its faddy and unnecessary and will disrupt our whole routine.'

'And we must have our routine at all costs,' Richard said drily.

She glanced sideways at him and saw that he was regarding her with a look that could indicate amusement, or something else.

'Obviously you think that's a petty attitude,' she retorted.

'Well, isn't it, Sherie?'

'I worded it badly, perhaps,' she answered snappily. 'I was thinking of ill-feeling created with other parents, all sorts of other demands that might be made in consequence. Half our parents wanting to bring in meals. Problems with health regulations…'

'At one hospital I worked at in Africa,' said Richard, 'there were no hospital meals. Patients' families brought food in every day.'

'This isn't Africa, for heaven's sake!'

'True.'

They had reached the lift area, where one or two other people were waiting. Sherie was about to make some polite farewell remark about seeing each other soon, in order to finish off the awkward conversation, but Richard spoke again in a deliberately low tone that no one else would hear.

'Don't feel bad about last night, Sherie.'

'I'm not,' she assured him.

'All right, if you say so, but you've been very prickly today.'

'I didn't sleep well last night.' She made the admission without thinking, and saw a light of satisfaction glow briefly in his smoky-blue eyes. How stupid to have said that! It was clear he thought that her mood today was just another stage in her therapy. Oh, why on earth had she given so much away to him yesterday?

'Fancy another outing at the weekend?' he was saying now, cool and so confident. Good-looking, athletic, successful in his profession…Sherie imagined he'd never had that confidence challenged. He'd probably spent all of his adult life in a sort of warm bath of adoration from girls like Alison Grace.

'Actually, I'm booked up,' she replied—not truthfully—to his casual invitation.

He nodded. 'Thought you might be…See you soon then.'

The lift had arrived, and he got into it with the other two people who had been waiting. He gave a last smile at her before the thick metal doors swept smoothly across. Damn his superiority! Thinking he could see through to her inner motivations like that! She disliked him thoroughly now.

He wasn't in her thoughts as she walked through the cool fresh night to her car at eleven that night. She lifted her face to a faintly sea-tanged breeze and saw that the hospital tennis courts were lit up. This morning's rain had cleared away, leaving the weather still cool and the air unusually clean. The courts would have dried off enough to play on several hours ago.

Two pale figures played energetically under the white lights, one tall and athletic, the other of a heavier, stockier build. There was a quick beat of running feet, the slam of a ball into the net, a grunt of dissatisfaction from the heavier player, then an ungrudging laugh.

'You've got me, Richard! Close, though—five sets, too. I had no intention of playing this long.'

'Me neither, Eleven o'clock!' Richard exclaimed as he walked towards the fence and threw racquet and balls down near his pullover. He looked out at the night and caught sight of Sherie, who was trying to hurry past unseen. She looked quickly into her bag, pretending to be in search of car keys, although in fact she already had them in her hand, and he bent down to pick up the ball can.

They did not greet each other, and a moment later, Sherie was past, hot now, although the breeze still blew refreshingly on her face, lifting a strand of jet black hair from her ivory cheek like a caress. Behind her, the court with its green wire fence was a cocoon of light in the surrounding darkness, and the cheerful, healthily fatigued voices of Richard and his companion sounded as they talked over the highlights of their match.

Sherie felt a sudden pang of longing and loneliness tighten in her throat. She could be very happy on a court like that with a man, breathing a little heavily, limbs loose in a white dress, wrist sore after the persistent hammer of racquet on ball, preparing to go home together and step laughingly into the shower to wash away the grime of their game.

Yes, be honest! That was the extent of the intimacy she wanted to find. She wanted to know every part of a man and have the right to caress it, and to nestle against it. She wanted to know what it was like to sit over an ordinary, comfortable meal with someone, chatting as they shared the morning paper, planning some activity for the day. She wanted to explore a lover's feelings and thoughts on any and every subject, to find out about the music he liked, the faraway places he dreamed of seeing.

At times she still felt like a prisoner behind this wall that she had made herself, and that yesterday's outpouring to Richard had only strengthened. How could she begin to break it down?

'Hi, Shezz!' Robyn came out of the kitchen when Sherie entered the flat, a cherry-red chenille dressing-gown covering her slightly too rounded figure.

Like Sherie, she had had an afternoon shift, but the drive from North Shore Children's was shorter than Sherie's drive over the Harbour Bridge. 'I've just made myself a hot chocolate. Would you like one? I can easily fix it.'

'Mmm, sounds lovely!' Sherie nodded.

'Aren't microwave ovens a miracle?' said Robyn. This one had been a combined Christmas and birthday present from her parents last year. 'Why don't you change while I'm doing it?'

'No, I won't bother,' Sherie decided.

'You look tired!' Robyn said accusingly a moment later, when she had put a mug of milk in the microwave and pressed the electronic controls.

'So do you,' Sherie answered, leaning in the kitchen doorway.

'Oh, I know,' Robyn yawned. 'I have been burning the candle at both ends, a bit. I feel I've hardly seen you. You look tense too…' She broke off, then added in a new indignant tone, 'I know why! It's Richard Brent, isn't it?

Oh, Sherie! And I haven't even asked.'

'It's all right,' Sherie shrugged.

'No, it's not. What kind of a friend am I? Oh, I could kill that man!'

'You'd better not, Robs,' Sherie said with sudden humour. 'It's not the same one.'

'What?' Robyn wheeled around from the cupboard from which she had been taking out the hot chocolate. 'I don't believe you!'

'Well, its true,' Sherie answered lightly, then took in a deeper breath. 'I confronted him with it, yesterday, and he said he'd never been to New Zealand in his life, he hadn't trained at Newcastle, and eight years ago he was in Africa.'

'Did he give you any proof?' asked Robyn, her brown eyes narrowing in suspicion.

'Proof?' The microwave pinged out its signal that the hot milk was ready, and Sherie took the tin of drinking chocolate out of Robyn's hand and stirred in a generous spoonful.

'Yes,' Robyn nodded, 'Of course, he'd *say* he hadn't been to New Zealand. He was probably afraid you'd sue...'

'*Sue*?' Sherie was incredulous, and Robyn shrugged, offended at the derision she heard in her friend's tone. She took a mouthful of her hot chocolate and walked into the lounge-room.

For a wild moment, the thought entered Sherie's head that probably Robyn was right...Richard Brent had lied, had twisted his dates and manufactured a fictitious history in medicine, but then reason reasserted itself and she laughed aloud.

'Robs, hasn't this got completely out of proportion?' She followed her friend into the lounge. 'I know he was telling the truth. We…' she paused, and an image of the intimate evening they had shared rose before her mind's eye. She was about to describe it to Robyn, but then her natural reticence came to the fore. 'We spent quite a bit of time talking about his life,' she said carefully. 'There's no way he could have been lying. He seems like…' Again she hesitated. She had decided today that she didn't like the *new* Richard Brent either, but there was no point in telling that to Robyn. 'He seems like a nice person.'

'OK, Sherie.'

'Why do you want to go on believing that I've been so badly done by?' Sherie asked curiously.

'I don't,' Robyn answered huffily, then burst out, 'Oh, I don't know, So much happens to you. And you're so attractive. There's no drama in my life…Perhaps I look for excitement too much through you.'

'What about Bernard?'

'Oh, yes,' Robyn answered, breaking into a sudden smile that illuminated her plain mousy features and gave them unexpected radiance, 'I'm sure we'll get married, and I love him, and I know we'll be happy, but…' her face fell again, 'it's so *safe*!' She pronounced the word with distaste.

'Don't underestimate safety,' Sherie said gently.

'Oh, I know. Ignore me—I'm being stupid. I think I'll finish this in bed.'

Robyn picked up the mug she had put down on a stereo-speaker and stalked off to her room.

'Goodnight,' Sherie said helplessly, then sat down on the couch to finish her own hot drink.

They seemed to be drifting inexorably apart. What would that mean about the flat? Could they continue to share? And would they grow together again in a few years when things had changed in their lives again? Sherie thought about plump, good-hearted Bernard.

'Marry her, you old slowcoach!' she whispered fiercely to the empty room.

Out in the Harbour, pathways of coloured light shimmered across the water and a late ferry chugged its way into Circular Quay. It was time for bed.

On Wednesday, Sherie had an afternoon shift, during which she didn't see Richard. Alison Grace commented obliquely and wistfully on his absence.

'Doctors don't really spend a lot of time on a ward, do they?'

Sherie hid a complicated smile and agreed that, no, they didn't. They had a lot to do besides visiting their patients in bed and chatting to nurses of their acquaintance. She was now convinced that Alison's crush was completely unrequited and would fizzle out harmlessly with time.

Then came four blessed days off. Her roster seemed to have been unusually heavy over the past two or three weeks. She had lots of plans for the time—the beach, the library, Christmas shopping. Her father was coming to dinner on Thursday night, and on Friday night a nursing friend, Christine, had a spare ticket for the Sydney Dance Company.

As well, there was some medical reading she needed to do. Last month's nursing journal had contained an important article on Paediatric Oncology, and she needed to read it again more slowly and carefully now that she had settled in on the ward.

Sherie was glad that Dad was coming over on Thursday night. They had a closeness that was no longer marred by the fact that she hadn't told him anything of what had happened during that year and a half when he was in Saudi Arabia. Oh, he guessed that things had taken place which had changed her, but she had signalled pretty clearly that it was easier for her not to talk about it, and he had respected that.

After all, it was only because she knew him so well that she guessed his own grief for her mother was still very real. He never spoke about it, and it was eleven years now. She was almost certain that he would not marry again, although he was still a very presentable-looking man—trim at the waist, thick pepper-grey hair and lively grey eyes in a face that was not too heavily lined.

His very successful career with an international oil company kept him busy and involved extensive travelling. In addition, there was his passion for music, which had brought him a circle of like-minded friends and a record collection that numbered in the thousands. Sherie saw him at least once a fortnight when he was in Sydney, and felt that his life was a well-balanced and happy one.

She hoped he had the same confidence about hers.

'Still enjoying nursing?' he asked on Thursday evening, during a pause in his appreciative consumption of the fragrantly-spiced Thai chicken curry Sherie had prepared.

Robyn was out again, and they were alone in the flat. Sherie would be returning to the ward the next day, and had passed her days off almost exactly as she had planned to do.

'You're always asking me that, Dad!'

He shrugged. 'Just checking. You know if you decided you wanted to take time off to study for something else, I'd support you.'

'I'm getting a bit old to switch careers, don't you think?' It was a light hearted objection.

'At twenty-six? I don't think so. If you're not happy, you must do something about it if you can.'

'Well, I am happy.' Sherie smiled, 'so there's no problem.'

'Just checking, I'm off to New York for three months just after Christmas, you see—pretty short notice. Have to make sure you can look after yourself while I'm gone.'

'Oh, Dad, I think I'll manage.' she assured him, adopting the same slightly teasing tone he had used.

'And is there anyone special in your life at the moment? Is that why you don't want to make any changes?'

'Oh, no, nothing like that at the moment.' Sherie forced a laugh, and he did not pursue the issue. It was a question he asked periodically in different ways, always very lightly and casually, never probing for a further reply. But she knew that her answer always disappointed him a little, although he never said so.

'But you're busy and happy?'

'Yes.' And it was true. 'I've been gardening quite a bit. I've got a vegetable patch in one corner of the main garden, and we should have some home-grown lettuces soon. As well as all the usual things like tennis and films and friends…'

He nodded slowly at this, then his expression changed and he started talking about an interesting documentary that was on television that evening. Would she like to watch it with him? They'd have time to run through the dishes first. It wouldn't end late, so she could get to bed and get plenty of sleep before her busy day tomorrow.

There had been many evenings like this in their lives over the past few years. Sherie had some knitting—a luxurious evening pullover of different textured wools—and her father smoked his daily pipe of aromatic tobacco. It was very pleasant, but she knew quite clearly, in spite of the assurances she had given him, and her own inner conviction that she was happy, that it was not quite enough.

CHAPTER SEVEN

WITH a squeak and a rattle, the medication trolley arrived at the end of the corridor. Sherie and Lisa Perry were at its helm, ready to begin the morning drug round. Helen Harris, now in bed one, was first on the list. She was talking volubly to Storm Sinclair in bed two as they entered with the trolley.

'I'm adopted, you see,' she was saying. The word 'adopted' struck a chord in Sherie as it always did, but she had grown accustomed to letting it slide by now. 'My real Mum couldn't keep me because she wasn't married to my real dad. He was someone famous—probably a rock star, American, I think, and my mum was an actress. One day she'll decide to trace me and she'll probably want me to go and live with her in Paris or London or somewhere.'

'Time to stop talking for a minute, Helen,' Sherie said cheerfully, and the little girl closed her mouth immediately and lay back against the pillow.

You had to get used to the way a child's face fell when the medication trolley came round. Kids on this ward didn't cry and protest and refuse to swallow or to hold out an arm for the injection the way a lot of children do when required to take medicine at home, but the look of resignation and dread on their faces seemed unnatural and uncanny by contrast.

Helen took her dose quietly, then lay with her eyes closed for a few seconds, before wriggling into a sitting position and resuming her conversation with Storm in a more subdued tone. 'Anyway, I reckon

110

that's what'll happen.'

Storm nodded slowly, her pale little face serious and big-eyed. For once, her father wasn't there, having gone to do errands in town. He would be back in time for Storm's lunch, he had said.

None of what Helen Harris had said was true, of course. Her physical resemblance to both her parents was quite marked, but she was at an age where to be adopted seemed glamorous, and she had a natural tendency to fabricate harmless stories about her life in this way.

Or were they harmless? Sherie saw that Storm was looking, wide-eyed and silent, at an invisible point in the air, clearly lost in thought. She had scarcely registered the presence of the drug trolley and the two nurses, and she was clutching the amethyst crystal that almost never left her hand extra tightly.

It was now mid-January, and Storm had been on the ward for several weeks. At first, she and her father had settled down into the routine of the hospital better than Sherie had feared. Since it was the Christmas period, things on the ward had been quiet, and many of their long-term patients had been sent home for a break, but now East Six was filling up again, and Sherie could sense that tension was growing.

Yesterday, she had noticed a whispered conversation taking place between Mrs Maxwell and Mrs Harris in the corridor outside the room which Storm shared with Cindy, Helen and Lucy King. Terry Sinclair had been at Storm's bedside, guiding her through a session of slow breathing and deep humming, and the frequent glances directed at him by the two women had made it clear that he was the subject of their discussion.

On the small cabinet beside Storm's bed, a meal of

'living plant foods' had been sitting, ready to be eaten when the meditation finished. The scene would have looked innocuous enough to a casual visitor, but Sherie had also heard Terry Sinclair haranguing other parents about their children's diet and treatment, and his almost continual presence in the ward was becoming more than irritating. If he hadn't had Dr Brent's support, something would have been done about it before now.

'OK, Storm, love,' said Lisa. Storm focused her gaze and made a face.

'Bleahh!' she exclaimed, but like Helen, took her medication quietly.

They moved on to Cindy, and Storm and Helen went back to their conversation, but more quietly now, as if they didn't want adults to overhear.

In the weeks that had just passed, nothing had changed in Sherie's personal life. Christmas and New Year had involved the inevitable social contact with Richard that came with staff celebrations, though these had been fairly hurried and casual affairs in the busy environment of this large teaching hospital.

It had been quite easy to avoid him at those times—to slip past with a drink of punch in her hand and a murmured apology at one gathering, and to busy herself with passing around plates of nuts and crisps at their own ward party.

He had been paged on that occasion after spending no more than five minutes in the festively decorated ward conference room, and Sherie had watched him go, telling herself that she did not feel a shred of regret.

She had caught Alison's rather bereft expression, however, and half-expected that Richard would return later, after he had dealt with whatever had come up. He didn't though.

Cindy and Lucy had been given their medication and Lisa and Sherie were just wheeling the trolley through the doorway ready to tackle the four patients in the next room, when Sherie caught some more of Storm and Helen's conversation.

'I think I'm adopted too,' Storm was saying.

'Oh, I don't reckon you are.' said Helen immediately, not liking this challenge to the uniqueness of her own fantasy background.

'I *must* be,' Storm insisted, with an odd desperation.

'Hang on a tick, Lisa,' Sherie's said in a low voice.

'What?' Lisa stopped and looked across at her in surprise. She had just been involved in kicking a stubbornly crooked trolley wheel.

'Just…fiddle about a bit, would you? I want to listen to this.'

'Oh, right,' Lisa's brow cleared, and she flashed a brief glance at Storm and Helen, then looked down at the patient list on top of the drug trolley and poked at it with a pencil, pretending to be studying it carefully. Sherie fiddled with capsule bottles.

'Why must you be?' Helen was asking.

'Well, Daddy says there's a reason why I've got leukaemia. That it's because I'm emotionally blocked about something. I'm harbouring anger and fear, and I'm not dealing with it properly. Or something happened when I was very little…'

'So, like, he thinks it's your fault,' Helen summarised bluntly.

'Yes, and I don't know what it is, so I can't work through it and cleanse it out of me like he says I have to, to make me get better.' Storm was getting closer and closer to tears. 'But, If I'm adopted, maybe that explains it. Maybe my real mother couldn't love me, or something, so I got an emotional block.'

'I don't reckon it's your own fault if you get leukaemia,' Helen said sceptically. 'It's not *my* fault.' She tossed her head.

'Yes, it is, Dad says. He's read books about it. He's got one that goes through everything that can go wrong with you, like with your ears and your feet and your lungs, and it says what causes it. I mean, it says the bad feelings you have that cause it, not what doctors say.'

'Don't you believe in germs and stuff?'

'Of course, I do! Gosh, you don't think I'm stupid, do you?' Storm said indignantly. 'But if I didn't have a blocked attitude, the germs—well, I mean the multiplying cells, they're not germs—couldn't get in and take control. But I don't know what my blocked attitude is!'

She lay back against the pillows and closed her eyes, holding the amethyst crystal tightly in both hands. Sherie and Lisa exchanged a speaking glance over their medication trolley and wheeled it out into the corridor.

'Oh, glory be!' exclaimed Lisa when they were safely out of earshot. 'The poor little kid…thinking it's her own fault! Should we say something?'

'I don't think this'll be solved with a few quick words from us, Lisa,' Sherie answered realistically. 'She loves her father. She'll go on believing what he says—and of course we don't want to destroy her trust in him either.'

'No, he's not a complete black sheep, is he?' Lisa nodded. 'He spends so much time with her, and he really is doing what he thinks best. It's probably up to Dr Brent. He's the one that got the meal thing OK'd but I'm sure he has no idea about this emotional block business!'

'No,' Sherie nodded, She saw from the way Lisa looked at her that the junior nurse expected her, as Ward Sister, to be the one to broach the subject with the paediatric oncologist. And of course she was right.

She had managed to work quite comfortably with Richard over the past few weeks. Her memory of the evening they had spent together had lost its edge of immediacy and freshness now, and that burning kiss on her doorstep had stopped reliving itself in her mind with its initial frightening realism.

'I'll talk to him about it as soon as I can,' she said to Lisa, then they continued uneventfully with the drug round.

'Dr Brent, before you go…'

'Yes, Sherie?'

She flinched. He wouldn't call her Sister Page, although she had been very deliberate in never using his first name. 'We need to discuss Storm Sinclair and her father, if you've got time.'

'What is there to discuss?' he asked coolly.

They were standing at the nurses' station, where as usual about eight things seemed to be happening at once. One phone rang, another was already in use, two patients were due to go down to Radio, and one was being discharged. Dr Brent had just finished his ward round.

'If I tell you what we're going to discuss, we'll have started discussing it, so do you have time for a discussion or not?' Sherie retorted, and somehow they both started laughing. There was an Alice in Wonderland kind of illogical logic to the question.

'I've got time,' he answered. 'But how much longer are you going to go on being busy at weekends?'

He asked the question in a low voice, under cover

of the general activity, and was already walking towards the ward conference room.

'What do you mean? You haven't asked if I...' Was he teasing?

'I haven't needed to. Every time I've thought of it, you've had an unmistakable 'I'm busy at the weekend' look in your eye.'

'Oh.' The directness of his words left her speechless.

'So are you busy *this* weekend?'

'Um—well, I've got an afternoon shift on Sunday...'

'But Saturday's free?'

'Yes, I suppose so, but...'

'Then don't you think its time we had an excursion of the Sydney Harbour fan club? Some of our membership are getting restive.'

'All right,' Sherie shrugged.

'A man less persistent than myself might give up.'

'A man less arrogant!' she bit back sharply. He only grinned maddeningly, and she spoke again. 'Why are you doing this?'

They had reached the ward conference room. Richard entered first, and following him through, Sherie shut the door sharply behind her.

'You need it, Sherie, if you want me to be blunt.' He turned to face her, seeming suddenly taller.

'What gives you the right to say that?' She was bristling with anger now, and she knew that her cheeks had flushed to a dark pink.

'No right at all,' he assured her cheerfully. 'Does it have to get down to a question of right?' Then more seriously, 'If you really do hate this, Sherie, of course we can drop the whole thing, but after that talk we had, and then...'

'Which I thoroughly regret,' she put in, before he could go on.

'Do you?' he demanded. There was a long pause.

'Actually, yes I do,' she answered, aware that he was still studying her, but unable to look up to meet his eyes.

'I'm sorry, then. We'll forget it,' he said slowly at last, then his manner changed completely, becoming crisp and professional. 'Now, what was it you wanted to see me about? Ah yes, Storm Sinclair.'

'We must do something about her father,' said Sherie happy to change the subject. 'Did you know she believes cancer has emotional causes?'

'Well, there is beginning to be some evidence that is does,' Richard countered smoothly. He was seated now, in a low green fabric-covered chair, and he gazed at her calmly beneath dark brows. Sherie sat too.

'Richard, you can't possibly believe that!' she exclaimed. 'How can a five or six-year-old...'

'Yes, you're right,' he interrupted. 'Perhaps I should have said that there's some evidence that cancer can be *cured* by emotion. That is to say, by a patient's own positive attitude.'

'That's a very different thing,' Sherie said. 'Storm believes that the fact that she has leukaemia is her own fault, and she's guilty and confused and miserable about it. Did you know that?'

'No, I didn't.' He frowned. 'What gives you that impression?'

'I overheard a very revealing conversation between her and Helen Harris this morning,' Sherie told him, then sketched it briefly. 'I've been against this whole thing from the beginning. The diet...Parents are complaining...'

'Not to me.'

'Nor to me,' she retorted. 'To each other, in corners, whispering about it, and building up resentment —and that's worse, surely?'

'Yes, it's not good,' Richard nodded, then uncurled his long limbs and went to the sink. 'Coffee?'

'No, thanks.' Sherie watched him in silence as he poured himself a large mugful. He was frowning, clearly wrapped in thought. He hadn't reacted as she had expected. Somehow, she'd thought he would refuse to listen to her and deny that there was a problem. She'd expected him to pull rank, and behave with the arrogance of Professor Thorpe. She had imagined herself having to muster proven evidence to support her assertions, including, perhaps, a long and traumatic interrogation of Storm herself. But, instead, he seemed to have taken her seriously straight away.

'It's not good,' he repeated as he returned to his chair. His dark hair was a little untidy now, where his long fingers had raked absently through it, and his pale blue shirt had bloused out a little at his trim waist.

'I've wanted to take an innovative approach to this job,' he said, speaking seriously and meeting her gaze frankly with his smoky blue eyes. 'I believe that there should be room to accommodate a parent's special wishes, but when something like this happens...It seems as if I've gone way too far.'

'Don't blame yourself, Richard,' Sherie put in quickly, surprised, even as she spoke, to hear herself coming to his aid.

'Of course I blame myself,' he answered impatiently. 'I was keen to put something like this into practice and I didn't find out enough about Terry Sinclair's beliefs. And it's scarcely going to help the career of any future ideas I might have. I'm very glad you told me this, Sherie.'

'But of course... a ward problem,' she stammered.

'And yet there are other ward problems that you haven't brought to me,' he said mildly, raising one dark and well-drawn eyebrow at her. 'You've passed them on to Sister Colton or someone else and I've spoken with them instead.'

'Oh heavens, Richard!' Sherie exclaimed helplessly, standing up. 'Must we always ruthlessly probe each other's feelings like this? What do we have here? Self-help psychotherapy?'

He gave a shout of laughter and she found herself responding, although it hadn't started out as a deliberately funny speech. For an answer to her questions, he only rose lazily to his feet and reached out a hand to pull her towards him, and before she knew quite how it had happened, she felt the firm muscles of his arms pressing into her back and the seductive, caressing touch of his lips against her hair, her forehead, her cheeks, and finally her slightly trembling mouth.

Within minutes, they had gone from being adversaries, facing each other like two fencers in a competition ring, to being united, wrapped together like two trees growing intertwined, each of which would fall without the support of the other.

Given the suddenness of Richard's action, perhaps it wasn't surprising that Sherie could not even begin to gather her defences against it. She felt her strength ebbing like fluid through her legs and into the floor. Her muscles were limp, yet her skin tingled and was warm as his palm cupped her jaw.

With a weak gesture of rebellion, she turned her mouth away from his kiss, but let her face sink into the warm scented curve of his neck, then felt him nuzzle her and start to reach for her hair, to coax the heavy waves from their confining coil.

'I hate this…' Sherie thought. 'I wish I hated it. I wish I could hate him.'

He had put a tiny distance between them now, just enough to allow him to trail the fingers of one hand down to the buttons that fastened her blue uniform in a long line down the centre. She was suddenly aware of leaping pulses inside her, and of demanding needs that threatened to surge up and blur her self-control dangerously.

'Stop!' Her voice was throaty and breathless.

His arms dropped, brushing the taut curves of her breasts, but he was still near enough to resume his too-expert caresses without a second's notice.

'Not the best place for something like this, is it?' His tone was light. 'Couldn't you change your mind about the weekend?'

His lips found hers again, nibbling her with tiny teasing movements, and his hand returned to her hair, succeeding in letting it loose. Sherie felt it tumble down to the middle of her back, and a strand of it fell over her face, black and lustrous, His own hair, she found, as she threaded her fingers through it, was thick but soft and smelt of musky almond shampoo.

He was kissing her now, his breath warm and gentle on her neck, and he was murmuring her name. The hunger within her grew rapidly, and her response was as passionate as any man could have wished for. She hadn't felt this with Mark last winter, and what she'd felt for that other Richard Brent had been adolescent—an infatuation of the mind, not the body.

What was this? It was the strongest physical response she had ever had. Was it only the physical release that any maturing woman would experience if she had been denying this part of herself as Sherie had? How could you decide something like that in the middle of this tumult of sensation? His hands were running down her back with rippling sensuous rhythms and the whole length of his athletic torso and hard thighs was pressed against her own more rounded form.

'Sherie, this is very unprofessional,' he whispered huskily. 'Wouldn't it just be easier if you said yes to Saturday?'

'All right, you monster!' Sherie broke away, breathless and hot. 'If that's the only answer that'll make you happy, what chance do I have?'

She really didn't know what she was feeling. He was smiling crookedly, and his firm lips, still only a foot away from her own, tempted her again. She could easily have returned to his arms.

'Good,' he said calmly, and ran a smooth palm along the line of her jaw, then kissed her again very briefly on her slightly parted lips. 'Good…I'll see you again during the week, but we might as well make a time now. Ten? I'll pick you up.'

'All right.' Sherie nodded.

'And don't worry about Storm,' he went on, suddenly serious. 'I *have* been too quick to experiment in this case, but I'll undo the damage.'

He went towards the door, smiled at her once more and was almost out of the room before she thought to ask, 'What shall I wear?'

Instantly the response came back, 'Comfortable shoes.' Then he was gone.

Sherie stayed in the ward conference room for a moment and twisted her hair into a rough knot which she fastened with pins and a ribbon-covered elastic on top of her head, then returned to the nurses' station. Richard was still there, checking through some notes and charts.

Alison Grace had arrived for an afternoon shift. As usual, she was earlier than she needed to be, and was leaning against the back of an upright chair, pretending to read a nursing textbook, but really studying Richard, with the usual spots of adolescent colour on her cheeks.

She found a question to ask him, and he turned to her willingly to give a serious response. Her thanks were fervent, and Sherie saw the hint of a smile touch Richard's lips. He was flattered by Alison's attention. Who wouldn't be? Alison was unusually friendly to Sherie over the shift change conference, after Richard had gone, and Sherie wondered at the change. She couldn't flatter herself that it was because of anything she had managed to do to win the girl over. Their relationship had been continuing as it had begun, with Sherie taking a calm, professional approach to her interaction with Alison, refusing to get angry, and over-looking several incidents of stubborn zeal and self-righteous disapproval of what the girl saw as slackness in others.

Yet today, Alison's gaze was fixed on Sherie with the earnest respect and attention that she generally reserved for Richard Brent. Sherie couldn't help smiling secretly about it, but she was a little surprised to find that the change continued for the rest of the week.

It happened, too, to be a week in which she saw little of Richard, which meant that Saturday's outing began to loom larger and more ominously on the horizon. Had she been foolish to agree to it? His kiss had frightened her with its power.

Saturday dawned a glorious day. The sky was cloudless, but a cool change during the night ensured that it would not be blisteringly hot. Robyn was away for the weekend with Bernard in the Blue Mountains so Sherie was alone in the flat as she dressed in a brightly patterned sundress of mauve and pink tones. She had got up far too early that morning, her sleep routine adjusted to the early shifts she had been on for most of the past week. She was completely ready now, and it was not even nine o'clock.

Breakfast? Somehow, she wasn't hungry. An orange juice and coffee would do. Preparing and drinking the two drinks occupied her till twenty past nine, and then there seemed little to do but sit and wait. It was hardly worth beginning any task when it would be interrupted so soon. The flat was quite clean and tidy—and anyway, she didn't want to risk marking her dress.

She didn't even have anything to read, having planned a trip to the library last night, but not managing to fit in in. She could have gone this morning if Richard hadn't coerced her into spending the day with him, and after the library, she might have done a bit of shopping and gone to her father's flat to check on his indoor plants.

By a quarter to ten, she was dreading the day, and wondering how on earth Richard had managed to talk her into it. And when, at five past ten, he hadn't arrived, she had decided not to go. The doorbell rang five minutes later.

'Sherie, I'm really sorry I'm late,' he said, as soon as she opened it.

'That's all right,' she answered.

'My mother rang from Newcastle, and…'

'Really, it doesn't matter, Richard,' said Sherie, then took a deep breath and went on, 'you see…I don't think I'd better come after all. I'm—I got up very early, and I don't think I'm feeling very well…' She stopped.

'Is this your bag here?' he asked.

'Yes.'

'And your sunhat?'

'Yes, but…' she stammered.

He faced her, his hands on his hips and his head cocked to one side. It was a position of challenge, but there was a twinkle in his dark blue eyes and a smile waiting in readiness at his mouth. He was casually dressed in canvas pants and a short-sleeved shirt, both in a pale olive that seemed to heighten the colour of his tanned limbs. He continued to study her, demanding an answer and clearly not satisfied with her defiant return of his gaze.

Sherie sighed. 'Where are we going?'

He grinned, satisfied, and picked up her bag, swinging it across by its leather strap and handing it to her. 'Darling Harbour to start, I thought, and then a late lunch at Doyle's followed by a swim at Bondi.'

'I'd better put in a towel and my costume.' She went towards the bedroom, and heard his voice behind her.

'If you're not back within five minutes, I'm coming in after you.'

Helplessly, Sherie smiled. Was he like this with everyone? Deliberately probing their sore spots, with that disarming grin of his firmly in place so that you couldn't be angry with his bluntness…? Or perhaps it was a policy he only adopted with her.

Darling Harbour was crowded, but they spent a pleasant three hours there, wandering through the Chinese gardens, examining some old ships moored in the water alongside the landscaped walkways, browsing around speciality shops and studying the sea creatures of all kinds in the up-to-date aquarium.

'Are you sorry I coerced you into this?' Richard

asked her as they stood in front of a display tank of tiny tropical fish. Special lighting made every colour glow, and the viewing corridor in which they stood was darkened to heighten the vividness of the world inside the tank.

'Are you *fishing* for a compliment?' Sherie returned wickedly, and he groaned.

'That was awful?'

'It was, wasn't it?' she admitted, and they laughed, then watched the tank again.

Sherie felt the warmth and weight of his arm around her, and couldn't stop herself from leaning her head down so that it rested on his firm shoulder. He squeezed her gently and they moved on to the next tank. Behind them, a little boy turned to his father and said, 'These fish don't live at the beach, do they? They live in Queensland.

The aquarium was full of families—it wasn't the place for a lover's promenade. It was disturbing how little of Richard's touch it took to make Sherie weak with longing and need, and with that need came a vulnerability that terrified her. As if he sensed this, Richard made no more attempts to touch her as they finished their tour of the aquarium.

'Getting hungry?' he asked her, as they emerged again into the white light reflected from the new buildings of the Darling Harbour complex, and the blue of the sky overhead.

'Actually, yes,' Sherie admitted. 'I didn't manage much breakfast this morning.'

'Not good,' he said. She made a face at him in reply, but he only laughed, then went on matter-of-factly, 'I made the booking for two o'clock, so our timing's just about right.'

Sherie loved the winding drive through the eastern

suburbs along New South Head Road. Bays came and went from view, and the Harbour was glimpsed from a hill at some points and skirted closely around at others. Magnificent houses peered out through some lush foliage-jacaranda, bougainvillaea, frangipani, Moreton Bay figs—and when the road narrowed up past the old suburb of Vaucluse, a white lighthouse appeared, a beacon on the green cliff top overlooking the sea.

They sat outside under a big coloured umbrella at Doyle's and ate fresh oysters squeezed with lemon, succulent scampi in garlic butter, and lightly crumbed bream with tartare sauce and a crisp green salad. A half bottle of champagne was too tempting to resist, although Sherie almost never drank during the day, and she felt it singing in her head and making everything seem light and perfect.

'I'm glad there's a breeze.' said Richard, when they had nearly finished their meal.

'Mmm,' Sherie nodded. 'And I'm glad we're in the shade.'

'Actually, you're starting to look sleepy, Sherie.'

She laughed and nodded guiltily. 'It's not that your company is boring me into it, though,' she said hastily.

'No, it's the combination of champagne and sunlight,' he answered, 'I'm feeling it too.'

Sherie looked at the wide blue eyes and alert mouth, and the long brown fingers that ran up and down the stem of his champagne flute. He didn't look sleepy, just lazy and contented.

'Perhaps when we've finished here,' he went on, 'we should walk up to the Gap to work off our lunch, then head down to Bondi for that swim. Save dessert for later.'

Sherie stretched luxuriantly and put her knife and

fork together on her empty plate.

'Mmm,' she answered, 'sounds wonderful. But I don't know about dessert at all.'

'Neither do I,' he nodded. 'This was all so good, I'd hate to spoil it with anything else for a good while.'

So they had plain black coffees and left half an hour later to walk up through the park, beneath palms and figs, travelling at a lazy stroll, and talking only when there seemed to be something to say. Although it had not been a conscious decision, each of them seemed to have put a ban on any subject connected with the hospital or with medicine. Sherie didn't know if anything had been resolved about Storm Sinclair and her father, and somehow she just didn't feel like asking about it today.

At the top of the hill on the high rock cliffs that overlooked the place where the Pacific Ocean met the quieter waters of the Harbour, the breeze was fresher and stronger, and they stood there for nearly half an hour, simply watching the way the deep green-blue waves crashed on to the rocks in a rhythmic frenzy of white foam. There had been silence between them for several minutes when Richard suddenly turned to her and said very quietly: 'What would you do if I kissed you, Sherie?'

The strength drained out of her instantly, and she answered weakly, 'I'd kiss you back, I suppose.'

'I hoped you'd say that.'

His arms, hot from the sun, came around her and she could feel the wind brushing his hair against her cheek. His lips tingled on her own, at first so lightly that the contact was like brushstrokes, then firmly coaxing her mouth to open slightly and respond sweetly.

'You're so beautiful...'

'No, please don't say that. Please!' It was the thing she always hated to hear from a man. She distrusted it. It was what the other Richard Brent had always said.

'What's wrong, Sherie? You *are* beautiful.'

'But I hate that,' she told him.

She had pulled away now and saw that he was frowning with narrowed eyes.

In the harsh sunlight of an Australian summer afternoon, fine wrinkles were etched clearly in his tanned skin, and a slight shadow was already forming on the lower half of his face since his last shave.

'Is that all I am?' she went on. 'That's not enough to keep a man interested in a woman.'

'Perhaps I'm saying it because it's one of the easiest things to say,' Richard answered slowly and seriously, as if he was thinking through his feelings even as he spoke. 'Perhaps men tend to hide behind a statement like that, because it's harder to find words for what they're really feeling.'

Sherie said nothing. His arms were around her again and she was trembling, but when he tried to kiss her once more she pulled away. What he had said was undoubtedly, sincere, but like a swimmer making up her mind to enter an icy river, she needed more time, Like a swimmer...

'Shall we go to Bondi?' she said.

They swam for a long time. The Pacific Ocean in summer was warm even on a day like today that was not at the peak of a heatwave. The water was a safe place to be. At times, Sherie was too aware of the masculine shape of Richard's tanned torso, and of his graceful energy in the water, which revealed a man at ease with his body and one who delighted in physical release. But mostly she herself was lost amongst the sensuous buffeting of foam against her skin, and the tangy, stinging caress of salt and sun on her shoulders and through her hair. It was already six by the time they emerged finally from the sea, and the light had thinned to a darker gold against lengthening shadows.

Sherie flung herself breathlessly on the bright beach towel she had spread out on the sand, content to let sun and air dry the sea-water from her tingling skin. Richard stretched out his towel nearby and lay on his side, propped up on one elbow. They were both silent for several minutes, although the loud music of waves and of shouting children and blaring radios meant that their lack of conversation was scarcely noticeable. Richard was the first to speak.

'I think I'll invite you sailing.' he said thoughtfully. 'Have you ever done it?'

'Not really,' Sherie answered. 'Just a little putter around the Harbour once or twice. Is that what you meant?'

'No, I mean a weekend up to Pittwater and back. You'll love it.'

'Will I?'

'You obviously love the sea,' he remarked.

'Yes, I do.'

'Then it's settled. Two weeks from now, Friday night, we'll be leaving. It's a boat belonging to a friend, and there'll be several of us.'

Sherie opened her mouth to protest that she hadn't agreed to the plan yet, but stopped. There was no real reason to refuse, she wasn't busy that weekend. The Saturday morning shift she was rostered for could easily be swapped with Judy or one of the other Ward Sisters on East Six.

Lulled by the relaxing day, she was actually too lazy to be on guard against Richard. It was looking likely, too, that he would ask her to continue this outing into dinner together, and perhaps then, if she was regretting her agreement, she could manage to wriggle out of it somehow.

His next words, after another silence, came as a surprise. 'I'd better take you home, I think.' He smiled at her.

'Yes, it's getting late,' she murmured, and scrambled to her feet immediately to dry off her hair a little more and slip the patterned sun-dress over her turquoise and white bathing costume.

Forty minutes later, she had said goodbye to him—he had not tried to touch her again—and was alone in her flat. What had happened? Obviously he had other plans for the evening. Sherie was shocked at how disappointed she felt. In such a short time, with that casual honesty of his, and that way he had of probing right into her feelings, he had become far too important.

Sherie spent the evening alone in front of the television.

CHAPTER EIGHT

THREE-YEAR-OLD Simon Holland looked pitifully small in the high hospital bed, and somehow even smaller when he was moved to the trolley that was to take him down for his second session of radiotherapy. His little face was pale, and made paler by the swathes of white bandage wrapped around his head.

His mother, a small sandy-haired woman who looked older than her thirty years, hovered nearby, rarely taking her eyes from her little son's face.

'All right, here we go, little mate,' said the Irish orderly, and he and his partner began to wheel the trolley out of the ward towards the lifts.

'See you back here soon,' Sherie said, half to the child's mother, and half to the little boy himself, although he was unable to respond in his present state.

She wondered how long Mrs Holland would be able to keep up the level of care she had been giving to her child. Ostensibly, she was sleeping in one of the small rooms set aside for parents, as the family lived several hundred miles away on a farm just outside a small country town, but in fact the room went almost unused, and Mrs Holland would snatch brief periods of sleep in a chair at Simon's bedside. It appeared that Mr Holland could not leave his farm, so there was no chance of him coaxing his wife to take some rest or leave Simon to go to Radio by himself.

It was clear to all the staff that Simon was the most serious case on the ward at the present time. Originally, he had been admitted to West Six, and a CAT scan had confirmed his local doctor's fears: there was a tumour in the left hemisphere of the brain. An initial biopsy had been performed, and then another large operation to remove a sizeable part of the affected tissue, but when long consultations had taken place between Mr Marzouk, the surgeon, Dr Ross, the consultant specialist in radio and chemotherapy, and Richard Brent, the paediatric oncologist, there had been dissension about what to do next.

After their conference, Sherie had spent a helpless hour with Mrs Holland, unable to give genuine reassurance. The doctors disagreed, radiotherapy was to be tried, Professor Thorpe would be brought in on the case as soon as he returned from his January holiday, and that was all that she could say.

Now, at her desk at the nurses' station, watching the little boy's trolley disappear, Sherie found herself giving thanks that Professor Thorpe was due back at the hospital tomorrow. In fact, she was actually hoping he'd make a surprise appearance today. It had happened before, apparently. He had returned from holiday two days early last year, unable to believe that his professional world could survive without him. And this year, perhaps he would have been right to believe that—although Simon's case might turn out to need a miracle that went beyond what Professor Thorpe could perform.

Sherie heard masculine footsteps approaching and looked up eagerly, expecting to see the familiar impatient and intolerant features of the much-disliked consultant—it was ironic that for once she should actively *want* it to be him!—but instead it was Richard Brent who appeared, and he was definitely *not* someone she wanted to see.

It was ten days since their Saturday outing together, and in that time her feelings seemed to have frozen. A part of her wanted to respond to him; a larger part of her was unable to. She knew she was being too cool with him when they encountered each other over work problems, but he had made no attempt to break through to the warmth he must know was within.

'I was right to pull back,' Sherie told herself.

'Simon Holland's just gone down to Radio?' Richard demanded of her without preamble.

'Yes, Mrs Holland went too. She'll drop on her feet soon if she won't let herself get some rest.' Sherie spoke briskly and did not meet his eye.

'I think Ross is handling this wrong,' said Richard. He spoke in a low tone, his dark brow furrowed.

He was leaning over the high laminex-topped bench that separated him from Sherie. Because she was seated, he towered over her, and she was forced to look up in order to listen to him, though it almost seemed as if he was speaking his thoughts aloud, rather than addressing her in any particular sense. He drummed the flat of his brown hand on the bench, then continued,

'But Marzouk supports him…Look, I've got a couple of patients to see here, then I'm off. I'll be at the University tomorrow as usual, but I want you to ring me there as soon as Professor Thorpe gets in … Are you on tomorrow morning?'

He looked at her directly as he asked the question, almost as if he had only just registered who she was.

'Yes, I am,' she replied awkwardly.

'Good, then I can rely on you. I like your hair done that way, by the way,' he added looking at the arrangement of tiny corn-row plaits. 'Suits you.'

The comment took Sherie utterly by surprise, and a tide of colour swept at once into her cheeks. Her guard had been down completely, as a result of his matter-of-fact manner, and she knew that her face must have taken on a foolish, helpless expression.

But fortunately he had turned away from her almost instantly and begun to walk towards the patients' rooms, so with any luck he had not seen the ridiculous effect of his words. She watched him until he disappeared, all her defences down and her body pulsing with feeling.

To think that a few words from him, a casual, meaningless compliment about the experimental style she had spent some time over last night, could have this intense effect upon her—and when she had a lot of work to do, too!

She heard the high, musical sound of Alison Grace's laugh in the corridor, followed by the resonant chuckle which she recognised as belonging to Richard, and felt furious and sick. Here she was mooning about him, cherishing an off-hand phrase, and he was already engaged in banter with someone else!

Sherie found herself waiting for the lift with Alison at the end of their shift that afternoon.

'Whew! It's been a tiring day, hasn't it?' the girl said easily. 'And I noticed you were in early this morning.'

'Yes,' Sherie nodded. 'I was worried about Simon and his mother.'

It was true, but it wasn't the whole truth. In fact, she had been unable to sleep, and had finally decided that it was pointless to keep trying. After a slow mug of hot chocolate at dawn, she'd finally drifted into the car at six, knowing she would arrive early, but feeling that at least work would distract her from destructive musings.

But Alison was nodding and frowning. 'Poor little baby!'

'He's three years old. He's not a baby,' Sherie blurted. She frequently had to remind herself of the fact. The boy was small for his age, and the fact that his name was Simon brought forth painful memories.

'Oh…yes, I just meant…'

'It doesn't matter,' Sherie said hastily and much more warmly, realising how odd her objection must have sounded.

'I don't think Richard is completely happy with his treatment,' Alison went on. She brought out his name caressingly and possessively.

'If Richard has told you that…' the name on Sherie's lips sounded awkward by contrast.

'Oh, I just overheard him saying something about it,' Alison put in quickly. 'He didn't tell me anything special.'

'Well, in any case, don't talk about it to people, Alison,' Sherie cautioned seriously but not unkindly.

'Oh, of course not,' said Alison. 'I'm very careful about all that. I just said it to you because you're involved.'

'But even people who are involved…his mother, for instance. She's been given the whole picture as far as we know it, but that doesn't mean that you can talk about it casually to her in a way that might create fears for her. It's very important not to use expressions offhandedly. If she heard that Dr Brent was "not happy with the treatment" she might start to think that someone was doing a bad job.'

'Yes, I see, You're right. I hope I haven't done any harm,' Alison nodded, just as the lift arrived, and Sherie's little lecture came to an end.

She wasn't particularly happy about the substance of it. It had actually been easier to relate to Alison in the past, when the girl was hostile, than it was now, when she seemed to have decided that Sherie was all-wise and all-knowing. She wondered at the reason for the change,

which had been reasonably sudden. She was to get an
answer to this question almost immediately.

The lift was crowded with visitors and hospital
workers, and Sherie and Alison were squashed together
into a corner of the left. Alison seemed fidgety, and as
soon as another conversation was in progress in the lift,
she lowered her voice and said to Sherie, 'Sister Page,
is it unusual—I mean, do doctors and nurses at this
hospital ever go out together'

Sherie concealed her surprise and answered the
question squarely.

'Sometimes, of course, yes. As in any other working
environment, if people are thrown together some of
them inevitably click in the right way. People are
generally pretty discreet about it, though.'

'What about doctors and student nurses?' Alison
asked again, and the words came out in an earnest
whisper. 'You see, I think I'm in love with Richard. I
know I am. I go weak at the knees when he walks past.
Do you think—I mean, I shouldn't be asking you, but I
thought maybe you'd noticed. Or maybe he'd said
something. Do you think I've got any chance with him?'

Sherie considered her reply for several moments. The
lift had arrived at the ground floor, and she and Alison
walked slowly down the main concourse to the front
entrance, the young girl frowning and eager at the same
time.

'To be honest, I think it's unlikely, Alison,' Sherie
answered carefully at last. 'Don't set your heart on
anything. Try and enjoy your work and keep up your
other friends at the hospital without thinking too much
about Dr Brent.'

She stopped, thinking it was best to be brief in giving
this advice. She'd known Alison had a crush on Richard
since his first day at the hospital. She still *didn't* know

how they came to be acquainted before that. But she was a little dismayed at how deeply the crush seemed to run, and that Alison was actually cherishing hopes of a serious relationship with the man.

Alison spoke, with an uplifted chin. 'Thank you, Sister. I'm glad you were honest. I'll try and forget about him now. I'd better get going or I'll miss my bus. Goodbye.'

'Goodbye, Alison…'

The girl had already broken into a coltish run and was out in the bright sunlight with red hair flying before Sherie had even reached the front steps.

'The court awarded custody to him and his new wife, and I get to have her at the weekend, so now she's in hospital, he's saying I can only visit her then. She told him I was there last night, and was coming again today and even though he says he's not coming himself…' Mrs Anson was upset.

Her voice came shrilly through the phone, and Sherie could only listen patiently, tactfully inserting the occasional question or comment. It did seem like a quarrel that was fraught with past bitterness, and her heart ached for the little girl, Kylie, another leukaemia case, who was at the centre of it all.

The important thing to do now was to contact the hospital social work department, where trained staff were equipped not only to provide personal counselling, but to sort out legal ramifications as well.

Mrs Anson had started to go over the same ground again now, and to bring up incidents from her failed marriage which provided clues about what was going on, but which Sherie simply could not get involved in trying to sort out. It wasn't part of her job, and would only create a greater mess.

'Mrs Anson,' she broke in at last, 'I'm glad you've told me all this, But I'm going to give you another number to ring…'

At that moment she became aware that Hindley Thorpe was standing impatiently near her, gesturing to her to finish her call. She nodded and smiled at him to signal that she was winding up the conversation, saw him turn away with a gusty sigh of annoyance, and looked around for another staff member who might be able to help.

But everyone seemed busy. Stephanie Dowling was on another line, the resident was on his way down the corridor conversing earnestly with the dietician, and various other things seemed to be happening. Taking all this in had occupied only a couple of seconds. Mrs Anson herself would scarcely have noticed the hesitation. Sherie continued:

'It's Maggie Smyth in the social work department. You'll find she's a very warm, sympathetic…'

There was a sudden click and the line went dead. Sherie looked down at the instrument and saw that Professor Thorpe's hand had come down sharply on the cradle that held the receiver. She was so angry she could not speak at first, giving the consultant time to bark, 'I can't wait for you to finish gossiping…where's Richard Brent?'

'Gossiping? That was an important call from the mother of one of our leukaemia patients!' Sherie fumed. 'How dare you assume that your problems are the most important ones on the ward? That mother was nearly distraught, and I…'

'Look, Sister, I'm not interested in an argument. You can ring this woman back. I want Brent in here as soon as possible. Ross and Marzouk will be arriving in ten minutes, and I want coffee for four of us in the ward conference room. And no interruptions. We'll be seeing the patient in half an hour.'

'What patient, Professor Thorpe?' Sherie asked frigidly.

'Holland, Stephen. No, Simon,' he barked.

'He's at radiotherapy, I'm afraid.' She still spoke coldly, but her heart had thumped when he said Simon's name.

'Useless!' Professor Thorpe hissed. Sherie didn't know whether he meant radiotherapy, hospital schedules, or herself. 'Now, just get Brent for me, and then you can ring your wretched mother back.'

'Dr Brent is at the University, as he nearly always is on a Thursday.' Sherie said distinctly and slowly. 'Shall I try to reach him there?'

'Yes, of course. Page him—ring him. Whatever. But tell him to be here in ten minutes.'

He walked heavily towards the ward conference room, opening a briefcase crammed with papers, books and folders as he went. Sherie shook her head helplessly. How could anyone be so insensitively arrogant and yet so brilliant in his field? She was still almost trembling with rage at his rudeness, but he didn't care a bit. His mind was centred on a vital case, and that was all that mattered.

With a final sigh, she reached for the phone again, got an outside line, and dialled Richard's number at the University research building.

'Dr Brent?'

'Sherie! Hullo!'

She ignored the apparent eagerness in his tone. 'Professor Thorpe wants you in the ward conference room in ten minutes.'

'Simon Holland, I'll be straight over.'

The receiver crashed down at the other end, jarring Sherie's ears. Richard had been infected with Professor

Thorpe's impatience at once. He hadn't even said a
token goodbye. After punching up Kylie Anson's
personal details on the computer, she dialled Mrs Anson
again.

'I'm so sorry about that…we got cut off and then I
couldn't get a line. Now, I was telling you about Maggie
Smyth…'

When Sherie finished the call, Alison Grace had
appeared nearby, studying some charts. Sherie
exchanged a casual smile with the girl, then looked up
at the belligerent shout of 'Sister!'from the door of the
ward conference room.

'Yes, Professor Thorpe?' she replied sweetly.

'Did I or did I not ask for coffee?'

'Um, I believe you *did* ask for it, actually, yes,' she
returned, pretending to consider the matter thoughtfully,
then added half under her breath, 'But, there's no need
to speak me like that. I'm not your maid!'

Alison giggled. 'That's just what I said to him when
I first came here, and you told me I shouldn't have.'

'Ah, but *I* didn't say it to *him*,' Sherie pointed out,
with a wise wag of her finger. 'I said it to *myself*.'

'True,' nodded Alison, laughing, then added
confidingly, 'I'm sorry I was so rude to you about all
that. I should have realised…Well, Richard says you're
a wonderful nurse, and that I can learn an awful lot from
you, and of course he's right, so now I am.'

'You are what?' Sherie queried absently. Richard had
praised her professional capabilities to Alison.
Interesting.

'Learning from you. I wish we weren't going back to
college so soon,'

'Yes, it's gone quickly, hasn't it?' Sherie said with a
smile.

Dr Ross and Mr Marzouk, the consultant oncologist

and surgical registrar, were already in the ward
conference room with Professor Thorpe, when Sherie
went in to prepare the coffee, and he was questioning
them with his usual ruthless disregard for social
niceties.

'But the scan showed completely clear in the right
hemisphere, as I understand it?'

'Radiotherapy…' Dr Ross began.

'In this case it's just procrastination, nothing more,'
Professor Thorpe blustered.

'You're suggesting that the entire left hemisphere
should be…' Mr Marzouk began hesitantly.

'It's been done before,' the Professor retorted.

'But…'

'Marzouk, I understand you're already talking about
further surgery in any case.'

'After a period of radiotherapy, I think we should do
another biopsy, yes.'

The Egyptian doctor's slight frown became a little
more pronounced in his defence against his colleague's
onslaught. It seemed that it wasn't simply nursing staff
who had to make allowances for the Professor's
manner!

Sherie squeezed her way past him—he was pacing
around the carpeted square in the middle of the
floor—as unobtrusively as she could, with her carefully
balanced tray of four cups, biscuits, milk and sugar.
Richard appeared in the doorway at that moment, and
to her annoyance, her hand shook slightly at the sight
of him, and the fullest of the four cups slopped a little
into its saucer.

'Brent!' Professor Thorpe barked, and strode over to
shake his hand. 'You support me, don't you?'

'Well, the reading I've done on two other cases
suggests…'

'Do you or don't you?' the Professor probed impatiently.

'I do, Professor,' he nodded calmly, standing very upright, his chin thrust confidently forward and his hands deep in his pockets.

Sherie had no further reason to stay. She smiled faintly at Richard—only because he had smiled first—and went towards the door, forced to brush past him. His pale blue shirt was open at the neck and his hair was slightly tousled after his hasty journey from the nearby University research centre, but the untidy casual look only emphasised his attractions and made her think of the sailing weekend she had agreed to. It was only a day away now. She had swapped her roster with Judy without giving a reason for her need to, but Richard himself had not mentioned the plan, and she was beginning to wonder if he was intending just to let it slide.

Gently, she began to shut the door behind her, but before she had done so, someone—Professor Thorpe? Or Richard?—had stepped across and given it an impatient shove so that it almost slammed against her. Immediately, she heard the earnest consultation begin again.

It was difficult to concentrate on her other work, Sherie found. She had been caught up in the drama of little Simon's future, and when the boy and his mother returned from the radiotherapy session, she wanted to say something about the conference that was still taking place, but she knew she must not.

It wasn't until after the shift change-over, just as she was about to leave, that she finally found out what was going on. The four doctors had spent some time at the child's bedside, then Mr Marzouk and Dr Ross had left, while Professor Thorpe and Richard talked to Mrs

Holland. Judy Colton was giving instructions to the
second-year student on her shift. Stephanie Dowling
had left, one or two other staff were busying themselves
around the nurses' station, and Alison was chatting to a
young intern—for once about something unconnected
with medicine.

Sherie was tempted to linger to hear the news about
Simon, if any decision had been reached, but finally she
decided she could not stay any longer, and she was
already heading down the corridor, when she heard
footsteps behind her and felt a light hand on her
shoulder.

'Sherie…' It was Richard. 'Time for a coffee?'

The suddenness of the invitation, after his easy
acceptance of her coolness to him over the past week
and a half, took her by surprise, and she could only
accept.

'It'll have to be just a quick one downstairs,' he said,
'I left things a bit up in the air at the research centre, and
I'll have to get back there and do a couple of hours' more
work.'

'Oh, fine,' she nodded, angry about the perverse
disappointment she felt at hearing this news. She hadn't
really wanted to have coffee with him after all, and now
she was disappointed because he'd made it clear that it
would only be a short one! What on earth was happening
to her?

They sat in the general cafeteria on the ground floor,
where staff at all levels mixed with hospital visitors, and
even patients themselves, if they were mobile enough
to have received permission to move about the main
hospital building.

It was a noisy place, and the standard of food was
typical of any busy place with a large turnover.

He made no comment to Sherie about the quality of

their environment, however, but simply led the way
with rapid steps to a table in the least crowded area of
the cafeteria, and quickly got out rid of a dirty tray that
still sat on the red plastic cloth.

'Comfortable?' he enquired absently as soon as she
was seated, then barely waited for her nod and smile
before continuing, 'It's all settled…they're operating on
Monday. I had to support Professor Thorpe, even
though in my line perhaps I should have argued for a
continuation of radiotherapy. I know David Ross felt I
was letting the side down. But in this case…'

'So what will the operation do?' asked Sherie,
although she had been able to gather a pretty good idea
of Professor Thorpe's argument as she made the coffee.

'Remove the left hemisphere,' he said.

He was still completely absorbed in the case, Sherie
could see. He was stirring his coffee absently, staring
down into the brown liquid, and his tanned face was set
in serious lines. Then he looked up, and she met the full
force of his smoky blue gaze. Her heart lurched
sickeningly and she felt uncomfortable in the stiff cotton
of her blue uniform.

Then Richard went on, 'It sounds ghastly, I know, but
it's worked in the past. When a child is that young, the
brain can perform miracles. Hindley thinks that the right
hemisphere will already have taken over some of the
functions of the left. His sister is Frances Masterton, the
neurologist…you may have heard of her. I didn't realise
that until this afternoon—but it turns out that, as a result,
he's pretty well up in that area. It'll be a while before
the complete picture is known, though.'

'They have therapy techniques now for encouraging
new neurological pathways to form in the brain, don't
they?' Sherie asked.

'Yes. The whole thing will be a long haul, but if we're

lucky, we'll have a pretty good idea quite soon after the operation about how successful it's going to be.'

'How soon?'

'As soon as his language ability can be tested…probably later next week. Generally it's the left hemisphere that deals with language.'

'Yes, so if he can speak after the operation…'

'We'll know that the right hemisphere is starting to take over.'

'Oh, Richard, it's…' She couldn't go on.

'He'll be over in West Six, of course,' said Richard.

'But I imagine we'll all find an excuse to pay a visit there sometimes,' Sherie laughed. 'How did Mrs Holland react?'

'Very well. She understands the situation, and she said that if it's necessary she and her husband will move to the city to give Simon the best follow-up therapy. I wish they could operate tomorrow, but Professor Thorpe wants to ring a couple of people overseas, and get some more information faxed over. He's sure about what he's doing, but he wants to go over it all with a fine tooth comb nonetheless. That man is thorough.' He shook his head slowly, then ran careless fingers through his thick hair.

'Thorough…and thoroughly detestable,' Sherie said wickedly, and was rewarded with a chuckle from Richard. 'Although I'm starting to get used to him now.'

'Most of it's bluster,' Richard replied. He had barely begun to drink his coffee, but now he picked up the cup and drained it in a few mouthfuls.

Three hospital cleaners gossiped at the next table, a blur of yellow at the corner of Sherie's vision in their rather garish uniforms, and a middle-aged couple smoked diligently behind Richard's right shoulder. The fumes wafted over in Sherie's direction, and she stifled a cough.

But Richard was speaking again. 'Anyway, Sherie, this isn't what I wanted to talk about.'

'Isn't it?'

'No. It's about the weekend.'

'Oh?' she said carefully.

'We seem to have been too busy to discuss it.'

'Mmm…'

'Not to mention the professional mantle you've chosen to wrap yourself in.' He shot her a piercing glance, covered by a crooked smile, and she stared down, crimson-cheeked. He wouldn't let her get away with anything would he? 'How about if I pick you up tomorrow afternoon at about five-thirty?'

'All right.'

He outlined the personal items she would need to bring, and Sherie found herself nodding to it all. Then as soon as he had finished, he got up to his feet, swept their empty polystyrene cups into a nearby bin and slid the tray into a rack next to it, his gestures firm and sure.

'I have to get back to the University.'

His impatience emphasised the tiredness in his face, and Sherie wondered about the work he did at the University research centre. How much of his time did he spend there when he wasn't at the hospital? Did he find enough ways to unwind?

But he had turned towards the exit now, and she could no longer see the expression on his face. He was nothing if not decisive when it came to finishing a conversation, Sherie thought.

'Shall I walk you to your car?' he was saying. 'It's on my way.'

'No, don't bother,' replied Sherie. 'I want to stop at the gift shop and buy a magazine. You're busy. Please go.'

'Fine. All right,' he nodded impassively, shrugging his shoulders casually.

'See you tomorrow.'

Slowly, Sherie wandered to the gift shop, not intending to buy a magazine at all. She kept watching Richard and his energetic walk, until, after his silhouette had stood out for moment in the large sunlit doorway of the main entrance, he had loped with masculine grace down the stone steps at the front and was out of sight.

He must have said something to Terry Sinclair, because the bearded man had been much more subdued on the ward over this past week, and whispered comments from other parents seemed to have lessened. It was frustrating not to know what had taken place, and Storm's behaviour told Sherie nothing as yet. The little girl had started her radiotherapy treatment now, and was quiet and listless most of the time. Was she still labouring under the burden of guilt that her father had placed on her? It wasn't the kind of thing you could find out by means of a casual question.

Sherie found some time the next morning to sit at the little girl's bedside. As usual, Storm was clutching her crystal, as well as the more comforting shape her soft synthetic fur 'possum puppet'. She had her eyes closed as Sherie approached, but then they flickered open and she smiled up weakly.

'Hullo,' she said.

'Hello, Storm, how are you feeling today?'

'Oh...good,' she shrugged, making a face. 'I'm trying to visualise this thing Daddy told me, but it's hard.'

'What thing is that?' asked Sherie.

'Well, he said if I could think of the colour red, and imagine my strong red blood cells like an army multiplying and multiplying and flooding out the bad white cells that there are too many of, then it'd help me get better. But it's tiring to think.'

'Yes, it is, isn't it?' Sherie answered, 'It's a good thing to think about, and it will help you get better, but you don't have to feel bad if sometimes you're too tired. Is it tiring for you to hold the crystal and the puppet?'

'Sometimes,' nodded Storm. 'But I love them. Look at the crystal. If you look in it, you can think you see different lands.'

She gave the precious object, warm to the touch from the warmth of her hand, to Sherie, who looked at it closely and glimpsed the purple fires of its different facets. She almost dropped it a moment later when Storm's small voice said, 'Hullo, Dr Brent. You were in the doorway for ages, I thought you weren't going to come in, but you did.'

'Hullo, Storm.' Sherie looked up. '…And hullo, Sister Page.'

'Hullo.' Sherie got to her feet. She had been sitting in the chair beside Storm's bed, where Terry Sinclair was so often to be found. He could be back at any minute, she guessed. 'Heavens, is that the time? I've got a million things to do!'

She assumed Richard would stay in the room, but it seemed as if he hadn't come to the end of the corridor to see a patient, because he followed her out and walked beside her to the nurses' station.

'So you think that imagining an army of good red blood cells will help Storm conquer her leukaemia?' he asked.

'There's evidence that positive mental images do help, isn't there?' Sherie said defensively. 'I thought you were a supporter of that.'

'I am,' he said smoothly. 'But, I didn't think you were.'

'I did some reading last week,' she confessed, 'after that talk we had. It certainly can't do any harm.'

'And a lot of accepted medical treatments started on that principle,' he finished for her. 'Good on you, Sherie.'

'What for?'

'For doing that reading.'

'It's part of my job, isn't it?' she said defensively. 'And I haven't had much of a change of heart. I still think it can do a lot of harm for people to believe they have complete control over their own disease.'

'I talked to Terry Sinclair,' said Richard, answering her unworded question. 'He was pretty shocked over what Storm had been thinking, and I'm sure it's tempered his zeal a little. His wife seems sensible...I talked to her at length by phone the other day. He's going home to Bellingen soon, and she'll be down for the next two weeks. We can't know if Storm is completely reassured. Perhaps she's still harbouring some secret fears, but I think both parents will be on the alert about it now...Anyway, see you tonight?'

'Yes,' Sherie answered, planning to add a polite, 'I'm looking forward to it,' but he had already gone, past the nurses' station and along to the opposite end of the ward. She didn't see him again before she left the hospital at three.

CHAPTER NINE

ROBYN was making a cake when Sherie got home at three-thirty; the warm, chocolate-tinted aroma of it baking in the oven greeted her as soon as she opened the door. Wonderful! The flat felt like a real home this afternoon. Robyn was so rarely there these days.

'Celebration?' Sherie asked from the kitchen doorway.

Robyn was whipping cream, standing back from the mixing bowl at an awkward angle and making frustrated sounds as she tried in vain to stop her large yellow floral apron from becoming sprinkled with tiny splashes. There was coffee brewing on the stove too.

'Oh, I just felt domestic,' she replied, looking up from her labours. 'Bernard's coming over for afternoon coffee.'

'Right,' Sherie nodded.

'You see, I've got this *feeling* that today's the day he's going to…Oh dear, where's the clock? Is it burning?' Robyn interrupted herself distractedly.

'Not unless it is in the oven,' Sherie replied mildly.

'The cake? Of course it's in the oven?'

'I meant the clock, You seemed to think it might be burning.' Sherie said, deadpan.

'I meant the cake. What on earth are we talking about, Sherie?' Robyn demanded in helpless confusion.

'I think some of us—naming no names—are in danger of becoming hysterical.'

'I think you might be right, Sister Page,' Robyn sighed, 'I just thought—you know—making a cake might get him round to the point.'

'You could be modern and ask him yourself.'

'I virtually have…Maybe I'm wrong and he doesn't want to at all.'

'Of course he does, silly girl! He's just cautious.'

'Don't I know it! Ver-r-r-ry cautious. But the way to a man's heart is through his stomach. Little does he know that it'll probably be the first and last home-made cake he gets!'

They both chuckled for a moment; Robyn wasn't big on cooking. She turned back to the cream and said, 'So anyway, that's the picture.'

'What time is he coming?' asked Sherie.

'About four. The cake's due out…' Robyn found her watch behind a chocolate-rimmed mixing bowl, '…in a few minutes, so it's still going to be hot when I put the cream on it and it'll melt.'

'The cake?'

'The cream. Do you think I should put it in the fridge to cool down quicker?'

'The cream?'

'The *cake*, Sherie Page, you infuriating woman, you're doing every bit of this deliberately!'

'I think it might sink if you do that,' said Sherie relenting.

'Might it? Yes, I suppose you're right…Oh well, perhaps I should serve the cake in bowls and we can each just blob a bit of cream on top, then it won't matter. You'll have some, won't you? You're not going out?'

'I'll have some, but I am going out later,' Sherie said reluctantly. 'In fact, I'm away for the weekend.' The banter about the cake had been the best and most light-hearted conversation they'd had for ages, and she was reluctant to break the mood.

'Oh, that'll be lovely! Where? Who with?'

'I'm going sailing up to Pittwater.' Sherie said neutrally. 'With Richard Brent and some friends.'

'Richard Brent? Oh Sherie!'

'What's wrong with that?' She was immediately on the defensive.

'I didn't say anything was wrong with it.'

'Your tone implied it.'

'Well, I think you should be careful. I mean, a weekend away with someone… Bernard and I didn't do that till we'd been going out together for eight months.'

'There'll be other people,' Sherie assured her.

'Still…Are you excited about going? You haven't mentioned it.'

'We haven't seen much of each other.'

'True,' Robyn eyed her suspiciously. 'You don't really want to go, do you?'

'Yes, I do.' But it wasn't convincing. She was in the grip of the reluctance she had felt on and off about the idea all along.

'Sherie,' Robyn said severely, 'If he just coerced you into this somehow, don't give in. Ring him up and cancel.'

'I couldn't do that,' said Sherie.

'I'll do it for you, I'll say you're sick.'

'No, I'll go. I'd better pack a bag.'

'Nothing could be worse for you than a man who tries to force the pace of the relationship,' said Robyn with energetic authority. 'You need a man who's willing to wait…'

'Like Bernard,' Sherie put in, with more than a touch of cynical wit. She knew she'd hurt her friend, by the huffy silence that ensued. Robyn was cleaning up her cooking equipment.

'Robyn…'

'It's all right, I won't interfere, but I think if you don't want to go, you shouldn't go, and that's all there is to it.'

Sherie said nothing. Robyn watched her.

'I really won't mind ringing up for you and telling him,' she said.

'All right,' Sherie answered at last. 'Maybe it's best. I have had doubts...'

'Give me his number,' ordered Robyn.

Sherie did so, and Robyn marched to the phone.

'I'll go and change,' said Sherie.

She knew she was being a coward, but stubbornly decided not to care, and changed into her old sarong, which was becoming somewhat the worse for wear now, after two-thirds of a summer of heavy use around the flat.

'What did he say?' she had to ask, emerging from her room to find that Robyn was back in the kitchen.

'I got his answering machine and left a message,' said her friend. 'Told him you had a migraine.'

'Which might be true by the time he gets the message.' Sherie said hollowly.

Bernard arrived, and the three of them ate Robyn's cake. Bernard's three helpings were an encouraging sign, as was his suggestion that the two of them go up to one of the Northern beaches for a sunset swim, followed by dinner: 'Something special.' They were gone by a quarter to six, leaving Sherie alone to brood over the prospect of her now-empty weekend...But not for long.

At six, the doorbell rang, and Sherie knew at once who it was.

'Have you packed?' said Richard, striding inside without waiting for any preliminaries. His blue eyes were cool as they raked over her bare shoulders and the sarong—slipped too low, as usual. Sherie decided she might give it to a charity clothing appeal after today.

'N-no,' she stammered in answer to his question.

Clearly, he wasn't even going to refer to the call Robyn had made, with its fake excuse.

'Well, you'd better start.' he said.

'I'll be five minutes,' Sherie told him.

'Good, we'll be late as it is.'

'Richard, don't be angry, I…'

'You've been catered for, and you're expected,' he snapped, then clamped his mouth shut again and turned to study the view, while Sherie went to her room, every step a reluctant one.

They didn't speak again until they were on their way across the Harbour Bridge, heading for Rushcutter's Bay. Sherie was the first to break the silence, furious with herself now for being such a coward and determined to get over it.

'Richard, how did you know I didn't really have a migraine?' she asked.

He turned his head to look at her and raised one dark eyebrow sardonically, shrugging shoulders that were clad in a sea-green and white striped T-shirt. 'I'd been waiting for an excuse from you for two weeks,' he said. 'I didn't think you'd leave it so late.'

'Robyn suggested…'

'Don't blame it on Robyn,' he interrupted.

'No, No, you're right.' Sherie sighed and frowned. 'You're an infuriating man, you know.'

'You're a *more* infuriating woman!'

Sherie laughed, and he joined her, dissipating the tension. There was something dangerously refreshing in being with a man who could zero in unerringly, it seemed, on Sherie's very thought processes. It was the danger that scared her off, and the freshness that made her come back for more. She couldn't have said what *he* got out of the time they had spent together.

'Look at the spinnakers,' he said. 'We'll be out there soon.'

It seemed to be a truce signal, so Sherie nodded enthusiastically in reply, then felt her heart lift. She wound down the window so as to feel the evening breeze. This *would* be exciting!

'Do you need a hand?'

'Er, yes, probably,' Sherie said uncertainly.

The problem was that the boat and the jetty didn't stay the same distance apart for more than a second or two. She reached out an arm to take the roughened hand of the middle-aged man who stood comfortably on the white deck.

The leap was easier than it looked. Ray Cranston judged just when the gap between the boat and jetty would be narrowest, then gave her hand a gentle tug and she was suddenly beside him, swaying a little, but perfectly safe.

'You haven't sailed before, Sher?' he asked her.

'Not really.'

'Never mind. You look like someone with a bit of taste for adventure, doesn't she, Rick?'

Richard nodded casually from his position near the mainmast. Ray was obviously a man who felt ready to coin nicknames after only a brief acquaintance. Somehow, though, his enthusiasm and general friendliness did inspire confidence in his skippering abilities, and Sherie felt sure that the weekend would run smoothly on the practical level. On the emotional plane, though, she wasn't so sure.

Ray heaved her overnight bag across and dumped it at her feet. 'I'll take this below in a minute and show you your bunk. Come and meet the others first.'

With the leisure to look around now, Sherie saw three agile figures making mystifying preparations in the bows of the streamlined yacht. She followed Ray up the gently sloping slip-proof deck.

'Cass, Steve, Ben, come and meet Sherie…'

The three stopped what they were doing and came forward. They were all tanned and cheerful, bare-legged in shorts, and looked completely at ease.

'My daughter Cassandra, and crewing friends Stephen and Benjamin,' Ray introduced.

'And that's the last time you'll hear our full names from him,' said Cassandra with a grimace.

'I like short names,' her father said defensively. 'I told your mother that Cassandra was a rotten thing to saddle you with, but she insisted.'

'Mum doesn't sail,' Cassandra said as a deliberately audible aside to Sherie. 'She hates it. I don't know how they've stayed married for twenty-two years.'

'It's *because* she doesn't sail that we've stayed married,' said Ray, overhearing as he was intended to. 'If she'd been under my feet on my darling boat every weekend, we'd have been divorced long ago!'

'But fortunately your prejudice doesn't extend to *all* female sailors.' Cassandra retorted. A natural sun-bleached and green-eyed blonde, she looked about twenty.

'Water tank full?' asked Ray.

'Yes, and fuel,' Steve replied.

'Cass, show Rick and Sher their bunks, then we'll be away.'

Celestial II was very well-equipped in spite of its relatively modest size, Sherie was to have one tiny yet clean and pleasant cabin on the port side, while Richard would have its starboard twin. Ray, Ben and Steve had beds that were made up each night from the long bench seats on three sides of the dining table.

'And I get the bookshelf!'

'The bookshelf?'

'Well, that's about how wide it is…No, I'm exaggerating. That's it' Cassandra pointed to a tiny cubbyhole tucked away in the bows. 'But at least it's private, and Dad *does* snore!'

She showed them cupboards, stove, tiny fridge, first-aid and other equipment stowed beneath the seats, the auxiliary motor controls. 'What passes for bathroom facilities'—which were actually quite adequate—and even a games box containing cards, dice and board games in case of stormy weather when outdoor activities would be impossible.

Sherie and Richard left their overnight bags on their bunks, then returned to the deck.

'Let's get going, then,' Ray was saying. 'Dinner at Manly.'

'Anything for me to do?' Sherie asked.

'No, just hang your legs over the side and enjoy yourself for now. We'll get you crewing tomorrow,' Ray answered.

Ben, Steve and Cassandra were climbing nimbly around in their sockless canvas shoes, detaching mooring lines, preparing sails, and starting the auxiliary engine which they would use until safely out of the marina. Richard was helping them, looking as if he'd done it all a number of times before, as well. Sherie was glad he was busy, and that Ray was showing no desire to thrust them together as a couple.

She did as Ray had suggested, and went up to the bows, where a firm aluminium railing allowed her to sit on the edge of the deck and dangle her legs down towards the water with a feeling of perfect safety. They were under way now, gently negotiating the last

corner-post of the marina jetties, and almost ready to
cut the motor and use sail-power alone.

It was a glorious evening. The full heat of the day had
ebbed away, and a magnificent sunset was rolling
slowly and majestically across the sky. Light, broken
patterns of high cloud changed in colour every minute,
and the wind on the Harbour was balmy yet strong
enough to push the boat along at an exhilarating pace.

At home before leaving, Sherie had changed out of
her ill-omened sarong into baggy denim shorts of a dark
apricot, topped by a white T-shirt sketched with Ken
Done's distinctive caricatured shapes of the Sydney
Harbour Bridge and Opera House. Following
instructions from Richard, she also wore canvas shoes
without socks, as the others did, and so it did not matter
that deliciously cold salt spray splashed at her bare legs
as the white prow of *Celestial II* cut through the deep
blue-green water.

The harbour was full of pleasure-seeking traffic this
evening, as well as ferries, launches and an enormous
oil tanker on it way out of the Heads, whose black side
slid past toweringly close to the tiny yacht at one stage.

'Who has right of way?' Sherie asked Steve a little
nervously.

'Here in the Harbour, they do,' he replied. 'The
shipping lane isn't all that wide, and they don't have the
manoeuvring ability that we do. But the general rule in
open water is that power gives way to sail.'

He broke off to shout a response to the order to
'Tack!' from Ray, and they veered at a ninety-degree
angle away from the impressive wall of the ship, their
sails cracking like gunshots as the boom swung across.

Manly, where they were to moor for the night, was
less than an hour away, so this evening's sail was a short
one, and they wouldn't leave the shelter of the Harbour

until the next morning.

'I want to mind the boat,' said Ray when they were moored at a jetty near the suburban seaside resort. 'So, I'll just make myself some sandwiches and have a couple of beers. I've had a long week at work, so I'll probably turn in early, but you lot would probably like to eat out, so go ahead.'

Everyone nodded agreement, and Sherie followed Cassandra's lead, changing into stone-washed jeans and leather sandals, then adding a quick brush of make-up to eyes and mouth and running a comb through wind-tangled hair. A silver necklace of plaited chain around her neck, and a light turquoise jacket of cotton canvas, made her feel as though she had successfully bridged the gap between the casual attire necessary for yachting, and the respectability of dress that a restaurant might require.

On coming across Steve standing on the wooden wharf still in his frayed-edged shorts and canvas shoes, she thought that perhaps she needn't have bothered, but the quickly-quenched flash of fire in Richard's eyes as he saw her gave her a frank moment of satisfaction that she didn't stop to analyse. She tossed her head, and felt the breeze lift some loose dark curls and brush them against her cheek.

Richard's eye was still caught by the contrast of colours that she presented...dark hair and pale honey-gold skin against the stark white of the T-shirt and the bright thread of silver around her slim throat. She wished he would look somewhere else.

When the five of them had bundled into a large bench-seated booth at a noisy and informal Italian restaurant, conversation flowed easily around the obvious topic of sailing. Steve and Ben answered Cassandra's demanding questions about their recent

participation in the annual yacht race from Sydney to
Hobart, the start of which was as much part of Boxing
Day in Sydney as presents under the tree were a part of
Christmas. The pair of enthusiasts seemed to spend
every spare minute of their time sailing, and had taken
the race very seriously.

'Even though we only came forty-seventh,' Steve
said gloomily.

Sherie sat rather quietly, content to let others do the
talking, and it was only as they returned to the boat after
the casual and unhurried meal of pasta and gelato
ice-cream that she realised she and Richard had not
exchanged a word the entire time. It didn't seem to
matter.

Back on the boat, in the warm lighted interior of the
main cabin, Ray was cocooned in a green sleeping bag
and absorbed in an action novel that featured a stormy
seascape and a very inadequate-looking vessel on the
cover. Cassandra was already crawling into her
cubbyhole, and Ben and Steve were preparing their own
beds.

'I'd like to get away early if we can,' said Ray, then
added a little sheepishly, 'There's no good reason to, but
it just feels…'

He groped for words, and Cassandra stepped in.

'Dad's secretly wishing he was about to sail off round
the world. Going out of the Heads at dawn makes him
feel as if he's off on an adventure. He's really only about
ten years old underneath that weathered hide.' she
finished cheekily, then pulled her blonde head quickly
into her tiny cabin.

It was only just after dawn when Sherie climbed a
little stiffly on to the deck the next morning. The main
cabin was already a hive of activity. Sherie knew that
any offer of help she made would only mean she was in

the way, so she had come up here to enjoy the first flush of the morning.

'We'll get going and get out of the Heads straight away.' Ray had said, 'The wind is good…And then we'll relax and have breakfast when our stomachs have had time to wake up.'

'And *before* they've had a chance to wake up to the motion of the boat,' added Cassandra, giving doom-laden emphasis to the words.

Sherie enjoyed her few moments alone on the deck. It was a perfect morning. The breeze was only slightly chilly, and as soon as the sun was decently up, it would be hot.

'Sandy, are you ready to do the genoa?' called Ray, clattering up the ladder from the cabin and on to the deck. Cassandra followed her father, and there was the brittle flap of sails going up to the top of their mast a few moments later. Ten minutes after that, they were on their way.

Ray was at the wheel, and the three young crew people were talking together as they responded to the occasional instruction from their skipper. It meant that Sherie was with Richard, who had also ended up at the front of the boat.

'Let's hope we don't get seasick once we get out of the Heads,' she said lightly.

'Well, I've never been seasick,' said Richard. 'And I have tested myself in that area a number of times, so I'm being optimistic.'

'Did you want to steer us out of the harbour, Ricko?' Ray called at that moment, and Richard turned away.

'Yes, all right.'

Sherie was disappointed to see him go.

By lunchtime they were at Pittwater. The morning's sailing had been by turns exhilarating, fascinating, and simply relaxing to Sherie. There had been the sudden increase of swell in the waves as they passed through the Heads—the twin cliffs that opened into the miraculously deep and sheltered harbour—and soon she had become accustomed to the irregular rise and fall of the small boat, although the rippling, muscular waves had been a little heart-stopping at first.

Then, when they had steadied on their course to the north-east, and were passing a continuing vista of Sydney's northern beach-side suburbs with their ocean-facing windows and lush gardens, a summer breakfast of fruit and croissants and coffee had been prepared and enjoyed. Sherie had her turn of steering, and also of tightening or releasing different ropes as part of the manoeuvre of tacking the boat in a zig-zag line to catch the wind. Finally, they had left the open ocean again and had turned into the sheltered waters of Pittwater, where they would simply laze away the rest of the day and evening, swimming, lying on the beach, and wind-surfing, surrounded by small holiday villages and the lush beauty of the Ku-Ring-Gai Chase National Park.

The other members of the party had plans already made for the afternoon. Ray was going to fish, while Cass, Ben and Steve announced that they would wind-surf.

'What about you two,' asked Ray, looking at Richard and Sherie. She flinched at the way his words seemed to give them the status of a couple.

'I'll give you a wind-surfing lesson, if you like,' Cass said to Sherie. She snatched eagerly at the idea.

'That sounds lovely! I've never tried it!'

'I might check out your fishing spot, Ray, if you don't think that I'll scare them off.' Richard said quietly. 'Then I might swim or surf.'

Perversely, Sherie felt a sudden brief stab of disappointment at the thought that he might be off with Ray on the distant rocky headland all afternoon.

Ridiculous, since she had been the one to latch on to Cass's offer in the first place.

Wind-surfing turned out to be an exhausting activity for the beginner, and at first involved more time *in* the water than skimming on top of it, as she found herself time after time trying desperately to clamber on to the fibreglass board again after losing her balance when the wind caught the sail and pulled it from her uncertain grip. But after a couple of hours, she felt that some progress had been made, and she had some exhilarating zooms across the water when she'd managed to angle the sail in the correct way.

'But I feel like a drowned rat, and I can hardly lift my arms,' she said breathlessly to Cass as she handed over the board. 'It's time you had a decent turn instead of just giving me little demonstrations.'

'OK, fine,' Cass nodded. 'You don't want to keep going when you're tired—you could get into trouble. What will you do now? Go back to the boat?'

'No, I think I'll put on some more block-out cream and a hat and lie on the sand.'

'There's an umbrella in the boat, under one of the bench seats, if you'd like that,' Cass suggested, and Sherie took her up on the idea, finding the red-and-white striped beach umbrella with no trouble and anchoring its long supporting pole into the clean golden sand.

She could not have said, when she came to full awareness with a start some time later, how long she had been lying there, half-asleep and feeling her body dry out and relax after the watery buffeting it had received. Nor could she have any idea how long Richard had been beside her, lolling lazily on one elbow and dressed casually in black swimming trunks and white T-shirt that made him look very tanned and healthy.

It was only as she rolled languidly from her back to her side on the large fluffy beach towel that she became conscious of his presence, opening her eyes carelessly, then suppressing a start as she met his cool blue gaze and lazy half-smile.

Abruptly she sat up and blinked as the strong sunlight bounced off the bright water into her unaccustomed eyes. Her bare legs were in the sun now, and felt far too hot, and her hair was stiff with salt. Some grains of sand trickled down between her breasts and started to chafe beneath her turquoise and white one-piece costume.

'Hullo,' she said, 'I'd better move into the shade.'

Her movement brought her closer to him, and although they were surrounded by the sounds of swimmers and picnickers, boats in the water and the rush of rhythmic waves on the beach, their world seemed very small and quiet.

She knew he was going to kiss her, and her pulses had already started racing in anticipation. 'It's just my body's response,' she said to herself. 'Why can't I control it? We're going to go over the same ground all over again —a kiss that feels wonderful and then days of regret.'

But he didn't kiss her. Instead, he simply reached out a hand and covered her own warm brown fingers. It was the best thing he could have done.

'Hullo, you two!' It was a cheerful Ray, again using the dual-person greeting that had made Sherie uncomfortable before.

'Caught something?' asked Richard, gesturing towards the polystyrene, ice-filled 'esky' that Ray carried.

The mood had broken with Ray's appearance, and

Sherie knew that a valuable moment had passed.

'Yes, a beaut tailer. We'll barbecue it in foil with lemon and garlic and herbs, and we'll all get a good-sized piece of it. Cass is about to go along to the camping-ground to rinse off, Sherie. Only cold water, I'm afraid, and out in the open, but it'll get the salt out of your hair, and I thought you'd probably want to go with her.'

'Yes—thanks, Ray.' Sherie scrambled to her feet immediately. The tête-a-tête with Richard was thoroughly interrupted now.

She left the two men and walked hurriedly towards the boat, glad to snatch a minute or two alone. She shook out her sand-filled but colourfully-striped towel as she walked, and realised that her skin did feel sticky with dried salt all over, and her head a little heavy. A cold shower and the chance to slip on the clean casual cotton-knit dress she had brought with her would be good.

'Great! Here you are!' said Cass. She was just coming up on to the deck in her red and navy swimming costume as Sherie climbed on to the boat after wading out to it through clear shallow water. She carried a towel and a change of clothing, and Sherie hurried below to get her own clean outfit.

'Have you had a good bake?' asked Cass.

'Mmm! Too much, probably,' Sherie nodded, not thinking of her sunny nap, but of waking to find Richard, warm-eyed and gentle, at her side.

It had felt good. Maybe he did want something real from her, and she could at last let it happen. This glow of hope filled her sun-drenched body with new warmth and energy, and she stood in the cold jet of the shower and laughed with Cass at the sheer pleasure of it rinsing the salt from skin, swimming costume and hair.

Later, with clean bare toes, her body loose in the simple sky-blue dress, and her hair combed back out freely down her back to dry in the late sun, it was the same—sensuous, relaxing, a mood of almost ridiculous lightheartedness.

When they returned to the boat, preparations for a meal on the beach were already under way. Sherie sat on the edge of the inflatable rubber dinghy which Ben and Steve had brought ashore, and sipped the long glass of cool fruit punch they gave her.

'There must be something for me to do,' she said. A fire had been started, Ben was starting to peel and slice potatoes for chips, and Richard had gone immediately to help him.

'You could slice some onions, Sherie,' said Cass, indicating another chopping board, and a plastic bag containing several large brown onions. Sherie got to work, enjoying the busy atmosphere.

Cassandra had begun to prepare the fish her father had caught in the mouth watering way he had suggested, but when everything was ready for cooking, the fire was still a hot blaze.

'We'll wait till it dies down to coals,' Ray decided. 'Too early to eat yet anyway. Let's relax.'

Sherie felt utterly relaxed already. She caught Richard's eye once and smiled at him, and it did not matter that they did not speak. It was easy to simply sit, sipping her drink and watching the fire. Some of the others talked, but there was no expectation that anyone be involved in the conversation if they did not feel like it.

Half an hour later, Ray propped the big metal barbecue plate on four bricks at four corners of the fire, and an appetising sizzle and savoury aroma began to drift up. When everyone had plates of food, it seemed quite natural for Richard to come and sit beside Sherie on the rubber dinghy, their clean toes digging into the sand in front of them.

'Everything tastes different, doesn't it?' he murmured to her, and she nodded and smiled, knowing he meant the food cooked and eaten out of doors, but thinking that tonight, for her, the comment included the whole of life as well.

'Especially the fish,' she said to him. 'I haven't tasted any so fresh for years.'

'You should do this more often, then.'

'Yes, I should,' she nodded, 'I love the sea, and I've enjoyed the experience of sailing. But, short of inviting myself along on a trip like this, I don't see what I can do about it.'

'Take sailing lessons. Persuade a friend to go shares in a boat with you. Give up nursing and go hitch-hiking around the Pacific on a dozen different yachts.'

'Now you're teasing!' she smiled at him.

'It's the kind of evening where any of that seems possible, though, isn't it?' he said. 'Possible…and desirable.'

There was a caress in his tone as he said the last word, which made it clear that he was thinking of the word's other meaning as well. Sherie felt her pulses leap. It was as if he had caught a glimpse of her abandoned mood and was encouraging its blossoming within her.

She leaned forward to accept another fried banana from Cassie, and felt the open neck of her dress slip off one newly-tanned shoulder. Then as she sat back, Richard reached out a lazy hand and adjusted it for her, his fingers coming into brief gentle contact with her warm skin.

The sun set in a wash of flame-gold and mauve in the cloudless west as they finished the long, lazy meal. In the distance, unobtrusively, were the sounds of campers and late picnickers, and yellow lights were beginning to show in houses visible on the opposite shore. It was after nine by the time the meal had been cleared away. Ben and Ray and Steve announced that they were going back along to the rocks to do some more fishing.

'Glenda will pack her bags and leave me if I don't bring something back tomorrow,' said Ray, referring to his wife with mock gloominess. 'She thinks catching fish is the only worthwhile reason for going off in a boat!'

Cassandra went on to the boat to write a letter in the clear light of the main cabin, but Richard and Sherie did not stir from the fire just then, in an unworded agreement that made Sherie exult at the closeness they were starting to find.

'Fancy a swim?' he asked, after a long interval, during which the coals from the fire glowed orange, bathing his face in a warm light.

'Sounds lovely,' said Sherie, feeling that the atmosphere was too thick with unspoken words for them to remain like this any longer.

'This is your gear here?' He turned to her turquoise and white costume and rainbow-striped towel, which had been stretched on the rubber of the dinghy to dry. She nodded in reply to his question. 'We can change here on the beach and shower the salt off again afterwards.'

Richard made no issue of the fact that they were undressing on the beach, and in fact it was easy to slip her costume on beneath the loose cotton-knit dress before she took it off. He was ready too, in the neat black trunks that emphasised his broad capable shoulders and trim muscular waist, and the regularly-patterned forest of dark hair that covered his chest.

'Not scared of sharks?' he asked teasingly as they each felt the first gentle ripple of cold dark water close around their ankles.

'I think our odds are pretty good, aren't they?'

'Oh yes…Of course, night-time is their feeding time,' he added after a pause.

They were far enough out to tread water now, and Sherie suddenly felt a vice-like grip around one ankle. She gasped and thrashed around for several seconds before his wicked grin told her that it was Richard's own feet that had imprisoned hers.

'You beast! You *horror*!' she broke out indignantly, and started to splash him furiously in retaliation, which ended in laughter on both sides and a mad chase through knee-deep water along the shore away from the boat.

'Yes, I'm a beast,' he admitted at last, under her onslaught of water. 'Dreadful! Unforgivable!'

'All right, we'll call it quits, then,' Sherie said breathlessly.

'Had enough?'

'Yes, I think so,' she nodded. It was getting chilly, and she wasn't swimming energetically enough to stay warm.

'Me too.'

They left the water and ran to their towels, each glad of the chance of a vigorous rub to warm their cold skins. But when she had thoroughly dried herself, Sherie stood a little self-consciously, wrapped in her towel. Somehow it felt more awkward to have to peel off her wet costume and put her dress on again than it had to don the costume in the first place. She stood there, unaware that her hesitation had communicated itself to Richard, until he spoke.

'Got a problem?'

'Not really.' She wasn't going to admit it to him,

anyway. A cloud slid majestically over the moon, and suddenly it was much darker. It wasn't an isolated cloud either. A change was coming, and there must be a wind higher up in the atmosphere, although it felt quite calm and sheltered here at beach level.

But even as this thought lay unfinished in her mind, she heard him murmur her name softly, and found that he had come to her, encircling her with his water-cooled arms.

'Sherie…Sherie…' The name in his deep resonant voice was a caress. His lips said the words against her own, and she was enfolded in the stirring rapture of his kiss before she could reply—if there had been anything to say with words. To Sherie at this moment, it seemed that actions said it all so much better.

It did not seem to matter how long she stood here in his arms as they explored each other. Every moment of it was sweet, yet an adventure at the same time. When he took an arm away from her to lay his towel in the bottom of the inflated dinghy and coax her to shelter with him there, she did not protest, and when, minutes later, he slid the thin straps of her swimming costume from her shoulders and down to her waist to nuzzle the full firm globes of her newly-released breasts with his lips, she felt a stirring that demanded fulfilment.

There was a chemistry in the contact between them that could not be denied, nor did she want to. The gentle, ever-present rhythm of the small waves on the sand became part of the increasingly absorbing rhythm of their bodies, and she wished that time and logic could be suspended for a while.

'Please let me tell you again how beautiful you are,' Richard murmured, his voice vibrating against her. 'I know it's unoriginal—but how can I be good with words at a time like this?'

Sherie stiffened a little, and he felt it.

'You're not going to object, are you? Please don't! Sherie…'

Warily, she relaxed against him again, knowing that the tide of their passion had been stopped for the time being, and not yet knowing if she would let it start up again.

'I know you've been hurt,' he said. 'I know every time a man comes into your life you think of Simon, and it seems to you as if you're going to be letting yourself in for the same potential disaster, but believe me, it needn't happen again. You have to learn to…'

'Don't lecture me about it!' Sherie said sharply.

'Sherie…'

'And don't say my name as if you're being patient with a four-year-old!'

She pulled away from him with finality, and felt the cold air tighten her throbbing breasts, which were pale in the dim light. Quickly, she scraped the salty wet swimsuit up to cover herself, thinking suddenly and inevitably of New Zealand.

Simon had been conceived like this, almost in the open, in a place where she had felt the chill of night air strike on her bare skin the moment she had eased out of that other Richard Brent's embrace. The whole thing had seemed beautiful at the time, so natural and right and elemental, but she knew better now.

What a fool she was to let herself get so close to the same scenario! She stood up, found her dress and ducked into it quickly, then wrapped her towel around her waist for added warmth. The night seemed to be cooling rapidly. Or was it only her own body?

Richard stood up too, and she saw that the dark hair on his forearms was stiff and upright with cold. He was posed tensely and breathing hard, struggling to regain control of his physical responses.

'I'm sorry,' she said. 'I should have…'

'Sorry isn't good enough,' he cut in harshly. 'I've had enough of this. Stop pretending to yourself that you need protection—you don't. You need someone to be tough with you. There's nothing wrong with you. You're not neurotic or crippled inside from the experiences you've had. You're healthy and you're ready to love. I think I've made it pretty clear in recent weeks how I could feel about you, if you'd let me, but you won't let me, and I'm damned if I'm going to waste any more time over it. You accused me once of wanting to be your therapist, but that's not true. It's you who is looking for a therapist, but you don't need one. You need a normal relationship with a normal man, and until you realise that…'

He shrugged hopelessly, an angry frown creasing his brow, then turned on his heel in the sand and walked back towards the boat, shrugging into his T-shirt as he did so and flinging a towel around his neck as he spoke.

'Richard…' Sherie began numbly. In a moment of revelation, she knew that he was right in everything he said, but he didn't stop and come back to her.

'No, Sherie, I'm sorry. It's too late for you and me now.'

The words were thrown back at her harshly, and there was nothing more she could say. Sherie heard the splash of water as he waded out to the boat, before she had yet had a chance to gather her own thoughts any further. The suddenness of his anger and her self-understanding had left her reeling and shaken.

One moment she had been cradled in his arms as he explored the smooth skin of her nearly-naked body, and the next moment he had gone, with a finality that she could not doubt for a moment.

CHAPTER TEN

THE SEA was grey and the swell larger than Ray had expected in the open sea the next morning. The change had come with a vengeance the night before, in the form of a wild storm, and Sherie knew she would have been terrified if they had been sailing instead of at anchor.

'It'll still be raining in the morning, I'm pretty sure,' Ray had predicted accurately, having returned unsuccessful from fishing, in time to haul the dinghy aboard and direct everyone in getting all their supplies stowed in out of the wet. 'We'll have to sail back in it, which won't be fun...Not dangerous, though. We might as well leave straight after breakfast instead of hanging around here shut up in the cabin.'

'What a disappointment for your first real sailing trip!' Cass had said to Sherie.

'The two of you could come on a day sail with us next Sunday if you're disappointed,' Ray had offered. 'We might head down to Port Hacking, try out the fishing there. After that, it won't be possible for a while—Cass and a girl friend are taking some time off work and sailing the boat up to Brisbane.'

'I'm rostered on, how disappointing!' Sherie had said, manufacturing regret. 'But thanks for asking me. It would have been lovely.'

'I'm tied up too,' Richard had put in matter-of-factly.

Halfway to the Heads at ten in the morning, Sherie found she could stand it inside the cabin no longer. Richard and Ben were talking about sailing, and Cass was holed up in her 'bookshelf' with a migraine,

173

probably the result of all yesterday's sun.

'Could I borrow your rain-jacket, Cass?' Sherie said quietly to the younger girl, and on receiving a wan 'of course', she put it on and slipped unobtrusively outside and on to the deck.

In spite of the rain-jacket, she was soon soaked to the skin and shivering, but she suspected that this was better than the seasickness which had been threatening earlier under the assault of her own mood and the cabin's slightly stale air.

After Richard's angry and unmistakable ending of their never-easy relationship, the rest of last night, spent playing Scrabble, had been torture, and it was a relief to arrive at Rushcutter's Bay.

'OK, drowned rats,' Ray said to Steve and Ben, who had been helping to crew as the boat negotiated the Harbour, 'we've still got work to do cleaning up, but Sherie, you're purple all over! You'd better get straight home.'

'I'm all right,' she assured him unconvincingly, realising too late that it had been inconsiderate to get unnecessarily drenched like this. It would look as if she was shirking the work now, and if they did insist that she leave straight away, Richard would have to come too, since they had driven here in his car. 'Isn't there something I can do?'

'Listen, we're used to this,' said Ray. 'The best thing you can do to help is for you and Richard to drop Cass off home, if it's not too far out of your way. She's not feeling a hundred per cent, and her mother will be cross if I keep her here while we do all this.'

'I'm sure that'll be fine,' Sherie agreed.

A few minutes later it was all arranged, and under these conditions, goodbyes and thanks were not prolonged. Neither was the parting from Richard

outside Sherie's flat made much of. Cassandra was still
in the car, and Sherie sensed that he was relieved about
it too.

'I've got to get a move on,' he said when he had
unloaded her things from the boot of the car. 'I've got
a family barbecue this afternoon. "Rain or shine", I was
told.'

'Don't let me stop you, then,' Sherie said politely to
him.

He raised one eyebrow and answered in a deliberately
enigmatic tone, 'I won't.'

'How was your weekend, Allie?' Trudi Gerstle asked at
three on Monday afternoon.

The staff of East Six were gathered as usual for the
shift-change, and were indulging in a preliminary
gossip before they got down to serious business. This
week, Sherie would mainly be doing evening work, in
contrast to the morning shifts she had been working
quite often of late. Trudi was a pleasant, broad-faced
girl who was Alison's counterpart on the outgoing shift,
under the guidance of Ward Sister Helen Trenerry, a
woman in her mid-thirties of whom Sherie was not
overly fond.

'Oh, it was just fabulous!' Alison exclaimed eagerly.
'We had a family barbecue, which doesn't sound very
exciting, but—well,' she blushed prettily, 'it just
managed to be wonderful!'

The words 'family barbecue' struck a chord in
Sherie's mind. It was what Richard had used only
yesterday afternoon as his excuse for hurrying away.

'Yes, you were really looking forward to it at work
on Saturday,' Helen Trenerry put in. 'You were in such
a daze about it that I had to remind you three times about
phoning the social worker. Some gorgeous man from

the hospital was going to be there…'

'Oh gosh! Now I'm going to be so embarrassed!' Alison clapped pink-tipped hands to her hot cheeks and laughed. 'Yes, he was there, and he stayed for—oh, hours. I thought he might leave really early, but he didn't!'

Sherie grew cold inside. It was clearly Richard that Alison was talking about. Until now, Sherie had dismissed the junior nurse's feelings as a painful and very real but utterly hopeless adolescent crush. But if Alison was so pleased about the event…And what had Richard been doing at a Grace 'family barbecue' in the first place?

'Well, I'm relieved to hear it went well,' Helen was saying sarcastically. 'After all the fuss, and all the talk about recipes for marinating kebabs and satays…'

'Did you try the tamarind in the peanut sauce?' Trudi asked.

'Oh, utterly delicious!' Alison exclaimed again. '*Everyone* said so!'

'Let's get on with it, shall we?' Sherie put in crisply. She didn't understand her own feelings, and wished she could simply put a lid on them.

'I can't be jealous of Alison Grace!' she was thinking wildly beneath the outwardly calm manner. 'Richard said it was too late. I don't want it to be—I'm in love with him. I don't want to push him away any more, but it's too late, and he's decided it's going to be Alison instead of me.'

But she had no time to keep on with the feverish pain of these thoughts. Having called the attention of the group to the fact that there was business to attend to, she had better start the ball rolling.

'Any news on Simon?' she asked, with a huge effort knowing that it was a subject that would command everyone's attention and cover her own turmoil.

'He'll be in post-op recovery by now,' Helen Trenerry told her. 'I've told everyone not to go over there. There won't be any news yet. I suggest you ring them in an hour or two and see what's happened.'

'But from a purely technical point of view?' Sherie probed.

'Fine, apparently,' was all Helen said. She was not someone who developed concern for patients who were beyond her immediate province, although she was dedicated and thorough on her own ward.

Other matters were quickly covered, and the outgoing shift trooped off home, leaving Sherie and her group to the afternoon and evening ahead. Sherie found it hard to focus her concentration, and as soon as everything was running smoothly, she left the ward in Lisa Perry's charge and walked across to the ward on the other side of the building that was almost East Six's twin.

She stopped to chat briefly to Barbara Lacey, the Ward Sister, whom she knew slightly, and explained her errand, then went to the end of the ward, where there was a four-cubicle post-op recovery and intensive care room which serviced this ward and the ear, nose and throat ward on the floor below. Simon's small form could be glimpsed through the glass panelling that shielded his cubicle from noise and disturbance, and to her dismay, Sherie saw that there was another figure besides the expected ones of Mrs Holland and the intensive care nurse at the boy's bedside—Richard Brent. But it was too late to retreat now. They had all seen her.

Soundlessly, she opened the door and entered the cubicle, which was crowded with so many occupants as well as the almost frightening array of instruments and equipment. Every vital sign was being monitored constantly, and the little boy's body was almost lost amongst the tubes and wires that connected him to these ultra-modern pieces of machinery.

Richard gave a terse nod of greeting, while Mrs Holland smiled a pale tearful smile. The intensive care nurse—plump and sandy-haired—whom Sherie didn't know, said very quietly, 'His eyes fluttered open a few minutes ago. He might wake completely at any time. Dr Brent's been here for ten minutes.'

Sherie nodded and said nothing. In this atmosphere, she couldn't ask questions. Perhaps it had been foolish to come. Her practised eye took in the information on the monitoring equipment. Outwardly everything had gone well, but...

Two blue eyes suddenly opened in the little pale face they were all watching. For a moment they seemed to stare sightlessly, then they focused on the most familiar presence in the room.

'Hullo, Mummy,' came a clear little voice. 'You're here! Oh, good!' Then there was a small sigh, a faint smile, and Simon had closed his eyes softly again.

'Dr Brent,' Mrs Holland whispered in a trembling voice, 'he spoke! Doesn't that mean...?'

'Yes—oh, heavens, yes,' Richard said, his own voice hoarse. 'It's far better than we dared to hope. If he's using language so clearly and so soon...'

He stopped. Mrs Holland had overflowed with silent, racking sobs of thankfulness, turning and burying her head in the nurse's shoulder.

'Simon—my Simon,' she was saying, her words muffled and indistinct. The sandy-haired nurse smiled across at Sherie and kept a sustaining arm around Mrs Holland's narrow back.

Sherie felt her own throat tighten unbearably, and

tears pricked behind her eyes. 'I'd better go back to East Six,' she managed to say, then turned and hurried out of the post-op area, knowing that her control could break completely at any time.

She had reached her own side of the building and was just passing the small counselling-room when Richard caught up with her. For the length of the corridor she had been fighting back her emotion, but at the sound of her name on his lips, she broke, and turned quickly into the counselling-room to take refuge alone. It was the fact that the child's name was Simon, and that he was going to be all right. Somehow, it had brought back her own anguish of seven years ago, and that anguish had to be released.

'Sherie, you're upset and I want to help. Please open this door…' Richard was rattling the handle of the door she had managed to lock behind her. For a moment she hesitated. Didn't she just need to be alone? Then suddenly she knew that she needed him, needed his arms around her, needed whatever soothing words he might have to give, in spite of yesterday.

Fumbling, she unsnibbed the lock, and he came in, frowning.

'Sherie…'

'I'm sorry…' She stopped. Those words two days ago had made him angry.

'Don't be.' But today he was gentle. He took her face in his hands and kissed her tearmarked eyes, then caressed her cheeks with his cool palms.

'His name is Simon,' Sherie said shakily. 'Isn't that silly? That was the name of my baby. I told you that, didn't I?'

'Yes,' he answered simply, then took her in his arms and held her, the warm length of his body a stronger and safer refuge than anything she had ever known. She did not question the fact that she was in his arms again, after he had said only on Saturday that it was too late.

She had no idea whether it was seconds or minutes that they stood motionless like this in the silent space of the small counselling-room, and it did not seem to matter. At first, her physical awareness of him was simply comforting. It felt inexpressibly good to be cradled in the supportive arms of a man she knew she loved, and to breathe in the warm musky scent of the clean skin at his neck. His cheek was pressed against her hair, and his hands caressed the moulded shape of her back.

But once her need for tears had subsided, she felt the nature of their embrace begin to change. Richard began to kiss her forehead, then her face, his mouth dry and warm and smooth, then he found her lips and parted them gently with his own, so that the sweet taste of each other was mingled together.

His hands moved more rhythmically now, finding the places where her body's shapes were soft and rounded and full. Sherie's own arms wound around him, then came up so that her fingers could comb through his thick, satin-sheened hair. She felt pulses and tides rippling and stirring within her, and became a completely willing prisoner of this new moment.

Just this was enough—just his arms, his warm chest, her name murmured on his lips, and the drumming feelings inside her.

It was Richard who broke the mood.

'This again!' he said, with a harsh laugh. 'I really didn't intend it.'

'It's all right,' Sherie began eagerly.

'No, it isn't Sherie,' he looked at her with mixed emotions on his face that she could not clearly read. 'because I meant what I said on Saturday night...I'd better go. I have an appointment in five minutes.'

'Richard…'

'No Sherie.' It was said wearily and patiently, and he had gone.

Sherie stood motionless in the small room, her ears and throat filled with a suffocating drumming. At first she wondered how she would manage to carry on, then the feeling was replaced with a deliberate anger. He had accused her of weakness on Saturday, of pretending to herself and to others that she was more vulnerable than she really was.

Well, she would show him just how strong she could be! She wouldn't avoid him. She wouldn't go distant and brittle when they came into contact, and she wouldn't spend her nights sobbing about it. She would behave normally, calmly, in a friendly way. She'd refer casually to the times they had spent together outside the hospital, and she'd say, 'Yes', to that blind date Robyn had been suggesting lately, with a friend of Bernard's. If it turned out that a relationship developed between Richard and Alison Grace, she'd be quite calm about that too…

This first part of her resolve was tested almost immediately. Standing in the nurses' station with Lisa Perry half an hour later, Sherie watched the redhead bobbing down the corridor to one of the four-bed rooms, and Lisa followed her gaze.

'Do you realise that girl has been *singing* while she fills in charts!' Lisa remarked.

'She's either a reincarnation of Florence Nightingale, and possibly an improvement on the original model, or else she's in love.'

'Probably both,' Stephanie Dowling put in, having overheard the quiet remark.

And Sherie flattered herself that she gave quite a respectable laugh.

CHAPTER ELEVEN

'HOW'S work?' asked Robyn, stretching herself luxuriously on the rather decrepit outdoor lounger that was placed in the cool shade on the balcony, and reaching for a second croissant and a third cup of coffee.

Sherie sipped her chilled orange juice, then said, 'Good, on the whole. We're going to lose the little Vietnamese boy, I'm afraid, but some of the others are responding very well to their treatment.'

It was a Friday, nearly five weeks after Simon Holland had had his major surgery, and Sherie spoke brightly, although thinking about work always reminded her too strongly of Richard Brent.

She was carrying out the resolve she had made, and somehow she thought he had guessed something of her new attitude. They were really getting on very well as colleagues and as casual professional friends, with frequent small exchanges of chat at the nurses' station, and an almost instinctive understanding of each other's attitudes to various patients and treatments.

The blind date with Bernard's friend had been a brief disaster. She would not be seeing Gordon again, and both of them were frankly relieved at it. He had been pleasant enough, but they just hadn't connected on any level at all.

Sherie and Robyn were both indulging in a late breakfast on their balcony before doing some shopping and preparing to start work at three. It was a glorious day in March—hot, but not unpleasantly so when you were being fanned by a refreshing breeze from the

Harbour. Summer was officially over, but Sydney was rarely cold and wet. Sherie's feet were bare, and she wore a simple open-necked cotton dress in soft pink and white, while Robyn was still in a red silk kimono that she had pulled from the floor by her bed when she first got up.

It was one of the few times they had really sat down together this summer. Sherie was aware that the lack of real talking between them would begin to take a permanent toll on their friendship quite soon. Then Robyn broke a small silence with some hesitant words.

'Do you know what, Sherie?'

'What, Robs?'

'Bernard and I are engaged!'

Of course it was wonderful news, at last, and somehow it did a lot to break the barrier that had steadily been growing up between them.

'You're off tomorrow, aren't you?' asked Robyn, after there had been a lot of enthusiastic discussion of wedding plans.

'Yes,' Sherie nodded.

'So am I. We thought we'd go to a late movie at the Valhalla Cinema tonight after I finish work. Bernard's bringing a friend—*not* Gordon, I promise!' They both laughed. 'Do you want to come? Do!'

'Well...' Sherie began.

'You can sleep in tomorrow, remember. Take some clothes and change at the hospital and meet us afterwards...' Robyn looked so eager that Sherie had to say yes, and once she had, she looked forward to the idea. The film would be light and uplifting, an escape...

Alison was singing as she riffled through some files in the nurses' station that afternoon. Sherie's shopping expedition earlier in the day had kept her own mood high as well, so it looked as if it might be a cheerful day

on East Six—especially since it was Friday. Richard had
changed his University research day to Fridays now.

'This is my last week before college,' Alison said,
somewhat out of the blue.

'Oh yes, of course,' Sherie nodded. 'It'll be strange
not to have you and Trudi around. We've got used to
you.'

She sipped the tea she had snatched the chance to
make a few minutes before, and looked up from her own
paperwork. No one else was around at the moment,
although there were voices along the corridor as Monica
Adams discussed a small problem with one of the new
interns.

'Sorry I was so icky at first,' Alison said with a
self-conscious laugh and a coltish toss of her bright
head.

'You weren't *icky*!' Sherie laughed.

'Yes, I was. I've been icky all summer. And just plain
idiotic.'

'Well, you took a while to get rid of a few mistaken
ideas about the way a hospital works, but everyone goes
through that,' Sherie began, but Alison interrupted.

'Oh, I'm not really talking about that,' she said. 'It's
just—well, no, never mind. I won't say anything or I'll
just embarrass myself even further. But do you know
something? I think I've grown up a bit in the past couple
of months, and it's such a relief!'

'Is it? That's good,' Sherie laughed again, a little
puzzled about what lay behind all this. Alison had been
about to confess something, that was clear, but what it
was, Sherie had no idea.

'I wish Richard was in today. I'd really like to see
him,' Alison sighed now.

Sherie froze in spite of herself. Was that the reason
for Alison's continuing cheerfulness? Making a

noncommittal response, she returned to her work, suddenly aware of an ache in the top of her neck. So Alison felt quite grown up, did she? Well, Sherie felt *old* today, and it wasn't a pleasant feeling!

But her spirits had rallied again by eleven when she finished work, and she felt a pleasant sense of anticipation as she went into the bathroom near the lifts to change. She had bought a new outfit today—black, satin-sheened evening pants and a boldly-tailored blouse in sapphire tones that matched her eyes.

Touches of silver jewellery at her neck, wrists and ears gave added sparkle, and just for fun, she applied a thin line of silver shadow to her eyelids in addition to her more usual make-up. Tiredness and staleness after her shift had ebbed away, and she felt ready for a long evening. Perhaps she might even persuade the others to go dancing afterwards into the small hours—or to have supper in Glebe Point Road at the very least. As long as Tom turned out better than Gordon!

She stepped out of the bathroom, ready to hurry down to her car and be at the cinema with the tickets by the time Robyn and Bernard arrived from their more distant workplace.

'Sherie? Sherie? Oh gosh, I hope she hasn't gone already!' It was the voice of Gillian Bishop, the Night Sister, and a moment later she came quickly round the corner. 'Oh, there you are—thank goodness!'

'What's up?' queried Sherie.

'It's Robyn for you on the phone…That's a gorgeous outfit.'

'Thanks,' Sherie smiled. 'But it seems as if I won't be needing it now.'

Her doubt was confirmed by Robyn's breathless and disappointed voice.

'I'm sorry, Sherie, but Bernard's not feeling well, and

I've suddenly had a crisis on the ward. Everything always goes wrong at the same time! They want me to stay on another couple of hours. Do you mind? We'll make it another night. Sorry I couldn't ring earlier, but really things here are…'

'It's fine,' Sherie assured her. She could hear several voices in the background, talking urgently. 'I'll let you get back to it.'

'See you tomorrow, lamb.'

It was disappointing. Sherie felt overdressed as she took the lift to the ground floor and walked out towards the main entrance. The hospital was quiet at this time of night, with no visitors and no day staff around. There were two figures standing near the doorway, however, and it seemed ludicrously inevitable that they should turn out to be Alison Grace and Richard Brent.

He was leaning against a pillar, dressed in dark-textured suit pants and a white shirt, a matching dark jacket slung carelessly over one shoulder. Alison was talking earnestly to him, still in her uniform, her slight shoulders very firm and her face tilted up to him.

What was he doing here at this time of night, on a day when he wasn't usually at the hospital at all? Judging by the way he was dressed, he had a supper rendezvous with Alison, and the first-year nurse had not yet had a chance to change.

Sherie nodded to the pair as she passed them, and couldn't help catching some of Alison's eager phrases.

'I've been such an idiot,' she was saying, using the same phrase she had used to Sherie only that afternoon. 'I'd made everyone on the ward think that you and I…'

At that point, Sherie moved out of earshot, the sharp click of her heeled black shoes on the stone steps drowning out Alison's words. She tried to push what she had heard out of her thoughts, since she had put a veto on brooding over anything connected with Richard Brent.

Her pace was quick along the asphalt drive that led to the car park—past those tennis courts where she had seen Richard and a companion finishing their game that night before Christmas. She still hadn't managed to play on those courts herself.

If only these heeled shoes weren't so noisy! Now that her evening was not to be prolonged, she just wanted to fade anonymously into the night and get home to bed. She had her keys in her hand and was almost at the car when Richard came up behind her, his silhouette haloed in pale bluish-mauve by the nearby overhead fluorescent light that shone over the car park.

'You're a fast walker,' he remarked, his chest rising and falling. 'I've practically had to sprint to catch up!'

'I'm looking forward to getting home, that's all,' Sherie replied, on the defensive instantly.

'Home? Do you always get this dressed up to drive home from the hospital at eleven o'clock at night?' he queried ironically.

'I was going to a film, but my friends cancelled at the last minute.'

'Bad luck!'

'Yes, it was,' she nodded briefly.

Why couldn't he just say goodnight and go? What was he doing here? Had he come to pick Alison up? Perhaps he was filling in time while she changed, then he'd go round to the main entrance in his car and collect her...

'Seems a pity to waste all that effort,' he said now. 'Would you like to have supper?'

'Why? Have you been stood up too?' So he wasn't going out with Alison tonight!

'Stood up?' he frowned, his eyes very blue. 'Oh, you

mean the clothes? No—medical dinner. Then I was called into Casualty to give a second opinion.'

'That's unusual, isn't it?'

'Complicated case—a long story. So what about it?'

'Supper? I don't think it's a good idea, Richard.' Sherie looked down at her keys, searching for the right one. He was silent for a moment, then:

'Why not?' he asked.

Another car cruised slowly past, humming in the cool night air. The lights of the city threw up a pale luminous glow into the hazy air. It was very quiet.

'You said yourself five weeks ago that it was too late,' Sherie said in a low tone. 'But there did seem to be some sort of chemistry between us at one time. Don't you think it's playing with fire for us to go out together? And I thought you were involved with Alison Grace now.'

'Involved with Alison? Did she tell you that?'

'It's been obvious. She walks on air every time you come on to the ward.'

'Sherie, she's my second cousin. I've known her since she was a baby, and she's always seemed like a frisky little ginger kitten to me. I've known she had a crush on me this summer, and…' He spread his hands helplessly. 'What could I do? I didn't want to hurt her. I had to let her down gently. And tonight, just then, when you saw us together, she was telling me how silly she'd been, and how she was over it now. As for it being too late for us…'

'Yes?' whispered Sherie.

She faced him, leaning against the side of her car and looking up at the face that was a dark silhouette against the lights of the car park. But he didn't continue. Instead, he reached a hand out to her hair and threaded his fingers through it, studying her with a helpless expression. 'I don't know what to say.'

'Well, I'm not going to stand here all night waiting!' Sherie retorted mockingly.

'Are you cold? Let me warm you…' He enclosed her in his arms and squeezed her tightly.

'Richard…'

'I know—you're waiting for some kind of answer. Shall I be honest?'

'Do you ever succeed in being anything else?' Sherie queried acidly.

'You mean I'm generally unpardonably blunt?' he teased. 'Sherie…' He was caressing her now. 'I've got "a past" like you have. I went to Africa with a woman who I was hoping would one day be my wife. Three months later she married a South African millionaire. So I know about disillusionment. We've got a long way to go. A marriage isn't made out of one moment like this.'

'Are you asking me to marry you?' Sherie asked, incredulous.

'I think I must be,' he confessed, drawing away from her a little and grinning helplessly. 'I hadn't planned to. Only last week I'd still sworn off you for life. Only now that I've said it…'

'You can renege on the offer if you like,' Sherie retorted. 'I wouldn't like to see you doing anything too rash!'

He studied her for a long moment, and she met his gaze with challenge in her eyes. She was sizzling all over, and felt stronger than she had in her life. He was a wretch—speaking his thoughts and his doubts aloud like this! But perhaps that was what marriage was about—sharing doubts as well as certainties.

'On the other hand,' she continued boldly now, 'if you hesitate too long, you're giving me time to decide to say no.'

Almost before she had finished speaking, she was in Richard's arms again.

'Don't say no, darling. Don't! Say yes,' he whispered against her ear. 'Right now—please!'

'Anything to get out of this car park,' Sherie murmured. 'Yes, I will marry you, Richard.'

'Good,' he said, kissing her, and sending leaping pulses all through her. Then, 'It's terrifying, isn't it?'

'Rather,' she agreed.

'It's lucky we're both in it together, then.'

'Very.' She loved this freedom to be a little ridiculous, but when he spoke again seriously, she loved that too.

'I want to do some more work for the World Health Organisation,' he told her. 'Do you think you'll be able to be part of that? I want you to…'

'Part of it?' she queried.

'It'll mean travelling, living somewhere else. Perhaps Geneva, perhaps New York, perhaps Africa again.'

'Anywhere you want to take me,' said Sherie, feeling fire ripple through her and a melting longing that would soon be fulfilled, 'I'll want to go.'

'Well…' he hesitated, distancing himself from her just enough so that he could look into her sapphire-toned eyes. 'Shall we start by getting out of this car park, as you suggested a moment ago?'

'That could be a good move,' she agreed.

Unwrap romance this Christmas

A Love Affair
LINDSAY ARMSTRONG

Valentine's Night
PENNY JORDAN

Man on the Make
ROBERTA LEIGH

Rendezvous in Rio
ELIZABETH OLDFIELD

Put some more romance into your Christmas, with four brand new titles from Mills & Boon in this stylish gift pack.

They make great holiday reading, and for only £5.40, it makes an ideal gift.

The special gift pack is available from 6th October. Look out for it at Boots, Martins, John Menzies, W.H. Smith, Woolworths and other paperback stockists.

ROMANCING THE PHONE

Win the romantic holiday of a lifetime for two at the exclusive Couples Hotel in Ocho Rios on Jamaica's north coast with the Mills & Boon and British Telecom's novel competition, 'Romancing the Phone'.

This exciting competition looks at the importance the telephone call plays in romance. All you have to do is write a story or extract about a romance involving the phone which lasts approximately two minutes when read aloud.

The winner will not only receive the holiday in Jamaica, but the entry will also be heard by millions of people when it is included in a selection of extracts from a short list of entries on British Telecom's 'Romance Line'. Regional winners and runners up will receive British Telecom telephones, answer machines and Mills & Boon books.

For an entry leaflet and further details all you have to do is call 01 400 5359, or write to 'Romancing the Phone', 22 Endell Street, London WC2H 9AD.
You may be mailed with other offers as a result of this application.